THE
QUARTER-PIE
WINDOW

THE QUARTER-PIE WINDOW

MARIANNE BRANDIS

with wood engravings
by G. Brender à Brandis

Tundra Books

Text copyright © 2003 by Marianne Brandis
Illustrations copyright © 2003 by G. Brender à Brandis

First published by Porcupine's Quill, Erin, Ontario, 1985
First published in this edition by Tundra Books, Toronto, 2003

Published in Canada by Tundra Books,
481 University Avenue, Toronto, Ontario M5G 2E9

Published in the United States by Tundra Books of Northern New York,
P.O. Box 1030, Plattsburgh, New York 12901

Library of Congress Control Number: 2002112849

National Library of Canada Cataloguing in Publication

Brandis, Marianne, 1938-
 The quarter-pie window / Marianne Brandis. – 1st Tundra ed.

Previous eds. published by Porcupine's Quill.
ISBN 0-88776-624-2

 I. Title.

PS8553.R29Q3 2003   jC813'.54   C2002-904623-8
PZ7.B7367Qu 2003

We acknowledge the financial support of the Government of Canada
through the Book Publishing Industry Development Program and that of
the Government of Ontario through the Ontario Media Development
Corporation's Ontario Book Initiative. We further acknowledge the
support of the Canada Council for the Arts and the Ontario Arts Council
for our publishing program.

Design: Cindy Elisabeth Reichle
Printed and bound in Canada

1 2 3 4 5 6   08 07 06 05 04 03

Contents

York

Upper Canada

1830

ONE

McPhail's Hotel

The October rain poured down on the town of York, darkening the late afternoon and making the street a sloshing, oozing expanse of mud. The wind slammed into Emma Anderson so that she bent her head and pulled her cloak tight. Her brother John, carrying their small bundle of belongings in one hand, grasped her cloak with the other and slogged along beside her. Just ahead of them, however, their aunt, Mrs. McPhail, walked as upright and sure-footed as though she had somehow quelled the storm in the space where she was.

They were on their way to the hotel that Mrs. McPhail owned but that Emma and John had never seen. In fact, the brother and sister had never even met Mrs. McPhail until about two weeks ago and before that had hardly been aware that they had such a relative. Now here they were in a strange town, under the guardianship of a brand-new and rather frightening aunt, walking toward the unfamiliar hotel that would be their home.

In all this alarming strangeness, Emma reviewed the few things that she did know. The hotel was a respectable one. She and John were to live there; John would work in a nearby livery stable and Emma herself was to be given a position in the hotel. *Surely*, she thought, *it would be a position with some dignity, as befitted the niece of the owner*.

Besides the fact of its being respectable, Emma knew nothing about Mrs. McPhail's hotel – her aunt was extremely reluctant to give information – but in her mind's eye she pictured herself at a desk keeping accounts neatly and with unfailing accuracy or, beautifully dressed, moving as the gracious hostess among the guests, their social and intellectual equal. She was, after all, the daughter of educated people even though she had been born and raised on a backwoods farm; soon she would be taking her rightful place as a gentle-woman. And, being rather tall, she looked older than her actual fourteen years.

But in the meantime she was wet, dirty, tired, and more than a little apprehensive.

Abruptly Mrs. McPhail stopped. She said nothing to Emma and John – she had not spoken to them since they had left the inn where the stagecoach had set them down – but prepared to cross the street. Having waited for a horseman to pass, and having nodded in response to his politely raised hat, she lifted her skirts slightly and picked her way across. Emma and John followed, glad that there was still enough daylight to enable them to see their way and step carefully across the muddy street from ridge to ridge. Even so, Emma's foot slipped into a puddle and a fresh ooze of cold water came in through her boot.

Having recovered her balance, she looked up in time to see her aunt ascend a few steps to the veranda of an impressive house. On a post in front of the building was a sign identifying it as McPHAIL'S HOTEL. They were home.

As soon as Mrs. McPhail opened the door, the sound of an angry voice rushed out at them. Mrs. McPhail stopped in the doorway, but Emma could see past her.

"But Mr. Walker," protested a middle-aged woman in black who stood behind a counter and wrung her hands, "it will take only a minute or two! If you would be so kind as to wait . . ."

"I certainly won't wait!" a gentleman declared. He was short and plump, and his many-caped overcoat, now very wet, made him look nearly as wide as he was high.

"Surely, surely. . . ," the woman urged distractedly.

"It's a disgrace! This hotel was recommended to me by someone who stayed here not two months ago. He said it was respectable and well run. Now I come here and find . . ." He made an angry gesture and began drawing on his gloves.

"Oh, Mrs. McPhail!" cried the woman behind the counter, half in greeting and half in lament.

"McPhail!" exclaimed the gentleman, turning and glaring. "Are you the owner?"

"Yes, sir, I am. Can I help?" As she spoke Mrs. McPhail stepped forward and shed her shawl and gloves and hat. In spite of her wet skirt and slightly windblown hair she looked attractive, intelligent, and reliable. Emma, although she disliked and feared her aunt, watched in reluctant admiration.

5

"I was assured that this was a quiet, well-run hotel," Mr. Walker said in the exasperated, dogged way of someone who has already stated his grievance several times. "So when I arrived in town this morning by the boat from Kingston, I sent a message asking for a room. I come here at the end of a day filled with business to find my room in the state in which its last occupant left it – bed unmade, basin full of dirty water. . . ." He gestured again and picked up his hat from the counter and his valise from the floor. "This is not what I had been led to expect. I shall go to another hotel."

Mrs. McPhail looked at the woman behind the counter. "How did this happen, Mrs. Delaney?"

Mrs. Delaney, her narrow face tense and frightened, said, "Sally left suddenly this morning. She told Mrs. Jones that she'd done the rooms. And she *had* done all the others."

"Mr. Walker," said Mrs. McPhail in a pleasant, forthright voice, "you see the situation. I'm extremely sorry that this has happened but we'll have your room ready for you in a few minutes. It's a nasty day to be looking for another hotel. If you will be so kind as to join me for a glass of whiskey in the parlor . . ."

As she spoke the last words she opened a door across the lobby from the counter. It revealed a parlor where a bright fire burned on the hearth and from which some welcome warmth flowed. A sofa, fire screen, and several chairs were grouped near it; beyond, at the far end of the room, was a single long dining table. Emma herself felt almost irresistibly drawn toward the fire.

The plump gentleman was clearly of two minds, and the other people in the lobby waited anxiously for his decision.

He glanced from the parlor fire to a window against which, just then, the rain clattered in a sudden gust of wind.

"You will find our whiskey to be of the first quality," said Mrs. McPhail. "Or perhaps you would prefer a hot toddy to take the chill out. As my guest, of course. We have a very special recipe, that I'm sure you'll appreciate."

Obviously he would have liked to persevere in his anger, to walk out of the hotel that had disappointed him, but Mrs. McPhail's promises of warmth and attention – and the bad weather outdoors – overcame his indignation. "Well, perhaps," he said, setting his valise down against the wall. He hung his hat on a peg and began taking off his gloves as he stepped into the parlor.

"I will join you in a moment," Mrs. McPhail said and turned back to the lobby, closing the parlor door but keeping her hand on the knob. The other hand, half-hidden in the folds of her dress, clenched and relaxed in a movement that Emma recognized and dreaded.

The face that Mrs. McPhail turned toward the little group in the lobby was controlled and expressionless, far different from the pleasant one that she had shown to Mr. Walker. Under the control, she was probably very angry.

"I'll hear the details later," she said. "First we must do that room. Which one is it, Louise?"

"Number Three," said the woman miserably. "Sally . . ."

"Not now, Louise. May I have my keys, please?"

The woman came around the end of the counter and laid a bunch of keys in Mrs. McPhail's outstretched hand.

"Thank you. Now, Louise, tell Mrs. Tubb to take clean water, hot and cold, up to Room Three. Then show Emma where to find what she'll need for cleaning the room. Emma, I'm sure you'll help with this. Take off your cloak and go upstairs with Louise Delaney. When you've shown Emma what to do, Louise, come down again and stay behind the counter."

"Clean the room!" Emma exclaimed when she grasped what her aunt had said. "I thought I would be working at . . ."

"This is an emergency, Emma. I'm sure you'll do as I ask. John, you go to the kitchen. It's that door beside the stairs. Take Emma's cloak with you – I can't have it lying about here. Louise, make sure that Emma has a candle. I'll come upstairs in half an hour to see that everything is satisfactory."

Then Mrs. McPhail went into the parlor; before the door closed, Emma heard her speak pleasantly to Mr. Walker.

There was a moment's suspended silence in the lobby. Emma felt John press a little closer to her; she herself was looking at Mrs. Delaney but thinking of her aunt and feeling fear and dismay clench her throat. This new life suddenly looked grim and ruthless and incomprehensible, totally different from the images that she had been formulating as shelters for her spirit, and she didn't know where she would find the courage to deal with it.

A minute later, as she followed Mrs. Delaney past a grandfather clock and up the stairs, her fears became more specific. Surely she wasn't going to be forced by circumstances to be a chambermaid, carrying chamber pots and dirty linen! She was Mrs. McPhail's niece, not some hired girl. But then, this was an emergency. At such a moment she couldn't refuse. She remembered the recent talk she had had with her aunt about the future, a talk that at the time had filled her with hope because it seemed to promise interesting and dignified work.

But her aunt had in fact made no promises. Mrs. McPhail was too clever, and Emma was at her mercy.

At the top of the stairs was a squarish hall with several doors, most of them bearing numbers. One stood open. "That's the room that needs to be done," said Mrs. Delaney, gesturing at it, but opening another door. "And this here's where the supplies are kept."

She held the candle that she was carrying so that it lit up the inside of a closet, which was in fact a small room. The light revealed shelves of sheets and towels and, below them, pails, brooms, a dustpan, and other cleaning equipment. "Dirty linen in that," she said, pointing to a large, covered basket. "You'll sweep the floor and wash out the utensils when Mrs. Tubb brings clean water."

Emma glanced at the woman beside her. Mrs. Delaney had frizzy dark hair, a narrow face, and black eyes. Just now she was clearly worried at the prospect of having to report to Mrs. McPhail on the period while she had been in charge of the hotel. Emma, who had herself suffered from her aunt's chilly displeasure and her ability to ferret things out, was sympathetic, though at the moment she was more concerned with her own situation.

"Well, do you think you'll manage?" asked Mrs. Delaney. "I've got to get back to the lobby."

"Certainly," said Emma, hoping that her voice did not reveal her apprehension and dismay. Without a further word, Mrs. Delaney thrust the candle into Emma's hand and went downstairs.

Left alone, Emma went to Room Three. She held the light high so that she could look around – and was revolted. The chamber pot had presumably been standing in the room all day stinking. The window was firmly closed. The bed was one mound of crumpled sheets and covers, and the pillow had been punched into an unattractive lump. Wet towels lay on the floor. The basin was filled with scummy gray water. As used bedrooms went, perhaps, it might be only slightly worse than average – or so Emma, drawing on her limited experience of hotels, supposed – but it was a stranger's mess. For years Emma had looked after the one large attic bedroom where her family slept and, all during this past summer, she had done those of the Wilburs with whom she and John had been living. But that was pleasant work compared to cleaning up after strangers who could leave a room in this state.

The only thing to be said for the room was that it was larger and handsomer than she had expected. Until now, the only hotel she had ever entered was the roadside inn where they had slept last night. In its attic, strangers were packed randomly, three or four at a time, into big beds or made do with some straw in a corner. The room where she stood now was spacious, with attractive curtains at the window, and with two bright rugs on the varnished floor.

Just then Emma heard heavy footsteps on the stairs. She went to the doorway to give whomever it was the benefit of her candle.

Toiling up the stairs into view came a squat, middle-aged woman, loaded down with two buckets of water, one of which steamed. She was wearing coarse clothes and had an expressionless round face with vacant eyes.

"Are you Mrs. . . . Mrs. Tubb?" Emma asked.

The woman stopped and glanced at Emma, then nodded and came forward. She set down the buckets in Room Three and was turning to go when Emma had an idea. Quickly she picked up the chamber pot and handed it to Mrs. Tubb.

"Please take this with you and . . . and do whatever is usually done." She had noticed a couple of clean chamber pots in the closet.

The charwoman gave her an incurious glance and again that single nod, then went away down the stairs.

Emma unbuttoned the cuffs of the sleeves of her dress and set to work, opening the window wide, dumping the dirty linen in the laundry basket in the hall closet, and shaking out the blankets. She emptied the basin into a pail that she found in the closet and cleaned it with some of the water brought by Mrs. Tubb. She remade the bed, put out clean towels, dusted the dresser that stood near the window.

While she worked, she kept the door open. She wanted to listen for sounds from elsewhere in the building and particularly for the approach of Mrs. McPhail. And indeed, while she was wiping the washstand there came hurried steps on the staircase. Emma looked toward the doorway; framed in it appeared, for a moment, a cloaked figure of a girl of perhaps sixteen.

"Oh!" the girl said and made as though to hide her face with her fur muff. Then she hurried on and entered another bedroom.

One of the guests, thought Emma as she resumed her work. The glimpse helped to give substance to her earlier imaginings. Already it was clear that Mrs. McPhail was right in claiming that her hotel was a good one; at least it was better than last night's roadside inn or the place here in York where the stagecoach had deposited them and where Emma had caught sight of a rowdy barroom. If Mr. Walker and the young

lady with the muff were typical guests, Mrs. McPhail definitely catered to the gentry. Emma had been looking forward
to meeting such people in York; here in the hotel she would
do so constantly. Her spirits lifted at the thought, even though
just then she was on her knees sweeping under the bed.

But abruptly her arm stopped in midmotion and she sat
back on her heels. What a fool she had been! Of course she
would not in any real sense meet the hotel guests. She would
be only a servant! The scene in the lobby came back to her
and she saw clearly now that Mrs. Delaney, though she was
evidently a sort of substitute hotel manager, had been in no
way Mr. Walker's social equal. Even Mrs. McPhail wasn't,
though she had a much higher standing. Mr. Walker had not
treated Mrs. McPhail as he would treat the ladies he met
socially. Each of them had a social position, but they were on
different ladders. Mr. Walker was a gentleman with, presumably, a clearly defined place on his ladder. Mrs. McPhail, even
though she owned a hotel, was not on his ladder but on
another one, along with tradesmen and servants. What then
of the chambermaid, who stood on the lowest rung of the
same ladder as Mrs. McPhail?

Had she really believed that working in a hotel would give
her any worthwhile contact with hotel guests or with other
educated ladies and gentlemen? In the backwoods settlement
where she had lived till now, the hard life largely smoothed
out social differences, though Emma had been perfectly aware
that her parents, with their educated speech, their interest in
books and ideas, were different from the neighboring farm
families. Here in York she would have to bear in mind that,
whatever her ancestry, her present social position was that of

a servant in a hotel. She might – she certainly would – observe the social life of the guests, but she could not share it.

With a sigh, she continued working and her mind reviewed the events that had led to her being here.

Seven months ago, in March, Emma's family home had burned down. She and John had escaped the fire but the rest of the family had not; the Anderson parents and two baby girls had been killed. Mr. and Mrs. Wilbur, across the road, had taken the orphans in until, in late September, Mrs. McPhail had come to claim them. Emma could not believe that that was only two weeks ago.

Up to that moment, Emma and John had forgotten that they had an aunt. Harriet McPhail was Martin Anderson's half-sister but over the years Martin and his wife had lost contact with her and the children had never met her. When making his will, however, Martin had evidently decided that, if anything happened to him and his wife, his half-sister Harriet was the only person to whose care he could leave any surviving children.

That was how Emma came to be cleaning a hotel room in York.

She pushed the floor sweepings into a dustpan and looked around to see what else had to be done. The room was neat and clean and fresh smelling now. The colorful quilt caught the light of the candle, and the pale varnished floor glowed softly. The wind, which would be striking the windows on another side of the building, was here only a rushing noise, hardly moving the curtains. Just as the earlier state of the room had dismayed her, its present condition pleased her and did something to reconcile her to her new life.

Taking the candle, she went to the closet and emptied the dustpan into a bucket that already contained similar refuse. She left the dustpan and broom exactly where she had found them and then, while rolling down her sleeves and buttoning the cuffs, looked around the closet again. Everything was neat, and the closet itself was spotlessly clean. Wary as Emma was of her aunt, and apprehensive as she was about her own future, she could still recognize this sign of Mrs. McPhail's good management.

As she was returning to wait for Mrs. McPhail's inspection, she heard voices and two pairs of feet on the stairs. In a sudden fright, she dashed into the shelter of Room Three but then, feeling foolish and a little inquisitive, looked back toward the open door in time to see two more strangers appear around the bend of the staircase.

The lady, who came first, was short and rather brown faced but pleasant looking. Her eyes were bright and her step, the way she shook back her hood, the darting glances, suggested energy. The gentleman, who carried a candle, was of medium height and spare, dark-haired and clean-shaven, and also with a weathered complexion. They were perhaps in their middle or late thirties.

Emma stood still and watched them. So far in her life she had not encountered a wide variety of people, and never before had she met so many in a short time except in her father's books. She liked the look of this couple – for they were certainly husband and wife – and her interest overcame her shyness so that she moved forward to stand in the doorway. She felt, oddly, as though she knew them, was already acquainted with them in some indefinable but important way, though of course she wasn't.

14

When they saw her they nodded pleasantly. The lady said, "Good afternoon. Are you a new guest?" She had an English accent.

As Emma was wearing a black dress and no apron, and as she was standing in the open door of Room Three, it was a reasonable question. Her heart lifted at this evidence that she did not look like a chambermaid. How she would have loved to be able to answer yes!

"No . . . ," she said falteringly, searching for further words.

"Come, Jane," said the gentleman. "You must get out of those wet boots." He gave Emma an agreeable look that was almost a smile. "My wife is a very obstinate person. She *would* come to the fort with me in spite of the weather."

Emma could think of nothing to say but she smiled at them. They were as friendly to her as if they were indeed old friends – though probably, she told herself, they were kind to everyone including chambermaids.

The lady gave her husband one of her bright, lively glances, then turned to Emma. "It *is* wet, isn't it? A real autumn storm."

She seemed about to say something else but just then Mrs. McPhail appeared at the turn of the stairs, the keys clinking slightly at her waist. Her expression was calm, but Emma, who had been learning to interpret that face, saw that her aunt was reading the situation and was displeased with it. Yet there surely couldn't be anything wrong in exchanging a word with guests?

"Good afternoon, Mrs. Heatherington . . . Major Heatherington. A wet day, isn't it?"

"Yes, quite. How was your journey?" Mrs. Heatherington asked.

"Very satisfactory, thank you." Mrs. McPhail smiled and nodded in a way that signalled the end of the conversation and drew Emma into Room Three, closing the door behind them. "Well, now, let's see how you managed. Gracious, child, close that window at once!" For a moment Mrs. McPhail's face twitched with irritation, but then it settled again.

Emma did so, but not without a word of self-justification. "It was so smelly that I just had to. You can't expect the poor gentleman to put up with . . ."

"No, of course not. But all that cold, wet air! And this is the only bedroom without a fireplace in it or next-door to it! Well, we'll have to leave the door open to let in some warmth, and I'll offer Mr. Walker a warming pan when he goes to bed."

Mrs. McPhail drew the curtains and checked the making of the bed, the cleanness of the water in the ewer, the state of the basin. Emma watched as tensely as though chambermaid's work was something that she was anxious to obtain rather than to avoid.

"You've done it very neatly," said Mrs. McPhail at last, and Emma was pleased in spite of herself. "Just a minute, what's that?" Mrs. McPhail slipped her hand under the overhanging edge of the washbasin. "A pencil stub?"

"Oh, yes, I'd forgotten. It was on the floor under the dresser. I wondered if . . . if I might keep it."

"*Keep* it?" asked Mrs. McPhail as if she had never heard such a ridiculous idea in her life. "Certainly not."

"It's only a small piece of pencil. I didn't think you'd return it to the guest who left it. I've . . . I've never had a pencil of my own."

"If you start keeping what the guests leave behind, whether it's worth anything or not, there's no saying where you'll end.

No. You may not keep it. If you find anything left behind in a room, give it to me and I'll decide whether to try to return it. Is that clear?" And she put the pencil stub in the pocket of her dress.

Emma, resentful and humiliated, nodded.

"And another thing. I will not have you talking with the guests, except about things concerned with our serving them. No personal chat. I don't know what passed just now between you and the Heatheringtons."

"It was nothing personal. Just about the rain."

"Very well. That is mere politeness and it's allowed. But nothing personal, you understand?"

Emma understood perfectly well. Mrs. McPhail wanted no one to know that Emma was her niece. What else she might be guarding against, Emma could not guess. But she realized that this prohibition would doubly isolate her from the hotel guests.

Reluctantly she agreed. She could do nothing else.

"Very well. Now you'd better go to the kitchen to wash. Tonight you and John and I will have dinner in my room and I'll explain what the arrangements will be after this. Come along."

TWO

Making Arrangements

Mrs. McPhail had a combination sitting room and office on the ground floor, across the lobby from the guests' parlor and next to the reception counter. The room was rather like the lady herself, uncluttered and a bit austere but dignified. A couple of rocking chairs stood by the fire, and a desk against one wall. A handsome tea service was set out on a side table and a piece of embroidery lay on one of the chairs. The two young people and their aunt dined at a round table that stood in one corner.

Mrs. McPhail had found time to tidy herself. Her hair, black with touches of gray, was once more in its two symmetrical wings above the smooth forehead. It was partly covered by one of her white indoor caps. She had changed into a dress that was not muddy around the bottom but was in every other respect identical to the former one, black with a row of buttons from waist to neck.

After saying grace and serving meat pie and vegetables from the dishes in front of her, Mrs. McPhail spoke.

"Let me explain first that we will not usually eat here like this. I normally preside at the guests' table in the parlor – Mrs. Delaney is doing it this evening – and you will eat in the kitchen."

Emma looked up from her plate, about to blurt out an objection. Just now, to reach the scullery where they were to wash their hands, she and John had hurried through the kitchen and Emma had shrunk from what appeared to be a pandemonium of noise, heat, frantic activity, and strange faces half-lit by the firelight. But she bit back her objection, recalling Mrs. McPhail's ability to take advantage of thoughtless words.

"That surprises you?" her aunt asked. "But you see, there is nowhere else."

When she thought about it, Emma realized that that was probably true. And perhaps the kitchen was not always such an unpleasant place. But still, to have to eat all her meals with the servants!

Then she remembered, with a little twinge of resentment, that she was a servant herself.

"John," went on Mrs. McPhail's cool, steady voice, "you will work for Mr. Blackwood as we arranged. You will sleep here – upstairs, next to Emma – and have your breakfast and dinner here. Mr. Blackwood will give you your midday meal."

John listened but said nothing. He had been unusually quiet, even for him. Now Emma saw that he was watching Mrs. McPhail with observant eyes but an unrevealing face.

Emma and John had met Mr. Blackwood, a large-voiced and well-dressed American who, a week ago, had appeared in the unnamed settlement in Flamborough Township that had been their home. He was, it seemed, an old friend of Mrs. McPhail's and had come there to look at the Anderson farm, with its burned ruin of a house, which Mrs. McPhail wanted to sell. Mr. Blackwood needed a boy to work in his livery stable and had agreed to hire John.

"John's clothes . . ." Emma began.

"Tomorrow afternoon you and I, Emma, and Mr. Blackwood will go to register the sale of your late father's farm to Mr. Blackwood. You will be present, as you requested. After that you and I will go to the bank to deposit your inheritance and John's in trust accounts. Then we will buy clothing for both of you at the stores."

"John should come with us for fitting, especially boots."

There was a moment's pause while Mrs. McPhail considered that.

"Very well, John will come along. For each of you we will buy one outfit for Sunday and one for daily wear. That will be a beginning. You, Emma, must be especially neat because to oblige me you will serve as chambermaid until I find another suitable girl."

"But . . . ," Emma protested, forgetting caution. "You said I'd . . ."

"You're quite right. I intend to employ you at other work when it's possible. But for now you'll fill the post of chambermaid. That means doing the guests' bedrooms each morning, and the upstairs hall, stairs, lobby, and guests' parlor. Once a week you'll clean this room and my bedroom. And you'll wait on table during meals."

"That's a lot!" Emma breathed.

"We rise at five o'clock. You'll do the downstairs rooms before breakfast, the upstairs ones after breakfast. In the afternoon, if you have completed your work and nothing else has come up, you will have a couple of hours of free time before dinner."

"I've done housework before but not waited on table."

"I'll show you tomorrow. As I will preside at the head of the table, you have only to follow my instructions. But you must be properly dressed." Mrs. McPhail gave a disparaging look at the dress Emma was wearing. It was the only one she owned, inherited from Granny Wilbur who had died a few days earlier, just before Emma and John had left home to come to York. The dress did not fit very well and was old and shabby, though neatly mended.

Mrs. McPhail offered second helpings. When she had served them, she continued. "I want you to have your new clothes before you appear in the dining room so I've asked Mrs. Delaney to serve at breakfast and luncheon tomorrow. You will serve at dinner, after we've been to the stores. When serving, you'll wear a clean kerchief and apron, of course. Naturally your dress will be black."

"Black!"

"Certainly."

Emma was silent but resentful. In her mind, black was Mrs. McPhail's color, or the color suitable for elderly people like Granny Wilbur. She herself was wearing it now only because she had nothing else. "Couldn't I wear gray, or dark blue?" she asked, as much to stem the inexorable stream of instructions and decrees as in the hope of gaining a point.

"No, it must be black. And let me remind you that your parents and baby sisters are only seven months dead. You should be in mourning for another five months at least. Besides, for someone with a small wardrobe, black is very practical."

Emma felt John's eyes on her and wondered whether she should protest further. During the past two weeks, ever since Mrs. McPhail had become a power in their lives, Emma had tried several times to resist. The trouble was that Mrs. McPhail had a knack of making her opinions sound right, or sensible, or at least plausible. She presented them as self-evident truths, and therefore she was especially hard to combat. A black dress would no doubt be both right and sensible, but Emma hated the thought of it. After her mourning was over, and in her free time, she would wear something colorful, like a blue-flowered dress that her mother had owned. She would think about that, and start saving for the material and planning how to design the dress.

Mrs. McPhail had, it seemed, more to say about Emma's clothes. "Of course you will always wear an apron while you are in the hotel, a large one for doing the rooms and a smaller one for waiting at table. An apron is like a badge of office, something of which the neat and efficient servant can be proud."

Emma said nothing. Aprons were not new to her; she and mother, and all the other women she had known, wore aprons during almost every waking minute of every day. No one saw any symbolic significance in aprons; they were just useful garments.

But obviously the apron she wore in the hotel would be still another barrier between her and the hotel guests. Even if the guests met her apronless outside the hotel, wouldn't they still regard her as a servant? Under that shadow, would she ever be able to take what she felt to be her place in the world?

So far as Emma knew, Mrs. McPhail never wore an apron.

Dinner was brought to an end with a cup of tea. When that was finished, Mrs. McPhail rose. The grandfather clock in the lobby had just chimed eight.

"I'll take you upstairs now, children. We've had a long trip and will be getting up at five o'clock tomorrow morning. Mrs. Jones, the cook, will wake you. Come along."

In the lobby they encountered several of the guests who had finished their dinner and were going out or up to their rooms. John moved among them with apparent unconcern but Emma was embarrassed by the shabbiness of her dress and her awkward social position. She watched two guests, a top-hatted gentleman and a lady in a furred cloak, say their farewells and leave – and at that moment she realized with a shock of discovery that she was not free to walk out of that door. She was a servant now and almost all her comings and goings would be controlled by someone else. As she watched the door close, she drew breath in ragged gasps and bit her lips to keep from crying out.

Major and Mrs. Heatherington were not among the guests in the lobby, but through the open door to the parlor Emma could see Mr. Walker standing by the fire talking to a lady who sat on the sofa.

While Mrs. McPhail had a word with Mrs. Delaney, Mr. Blackwood came from the parlor. He was a bachelor and, Emma had learned during their two-day-long trip, often dined at the hotel. Now he greeted them in his big Yankee voice.

"Recovered from your trip, then?" he boomed at Emma.

"Yes, Mr. Blackwood," she said, aware of a few curious glances from the dispersing guests.

"Fine! And you, young man, I'll be seeing you in the morning with your sleeves rolled up, eh?"

"Yes, sir."

"That's just fine! Well, then, I'll be on my way. Good night, all!"

Emma and John followed their aunt up the stairs, through a door, and up another flight to the attic.

"Mrs. Jones, the cook, also sleeps up here," said Mrs. McPhail. "The Tubbs are in the loft above the kitchen."

Most of the attic was open space with some old furniture piled in it. At one end, two rooms had been partitioned off. "That's Mrs. Jones' room," said Mrs. McPhail, pointing to the right-hand one. "This is yours, Emma. It was, of course, occupied by Sally, the girl who left this morning."

She opened the door. The bed had not been made nor the chamber pot emptied.

"Well, it won't take you long to put such a small room to rights. But you'll have to use Sally's sheets until wash day. I'm glad to see that she left the aprons." She pointed at two white piles on a shelf.

It was a tiny room, containing only the bed and a small table for the washbasin. Against one wall were pegs for clothes, and there were several shelves. The one window, in the far wall, was shaped like a quarter of a pie. Earlier today, on their journey toward York, they had passed a house that had two such windows set in a symmetrical pair high under the eaves. Now she had a room with one! Emma was too tired and tense to cheer up much, but she felt that the oddly shaped window would come to be one of her small pleasures.

The undeclared wrestling with Mrs. McPhail was not over yet. "Where is John's room?" Emma asked. "You said it was next to mine."

"He'll sleep on a pallet in the attic," Mrs. McPhail said, gesturing at the unpartitioned space. "There should be one already stuffed with straw – we had a guest's manservant sleeping up here not long ago." She strode across and prodded a large, flat sack, making it rustle. "Yes, that's it. And there's your washstand, John." Among the pieces of discarded furniture were indeed a table, basin, and ewer. In the wall above the pallet were two more quarter-pie windows.

"What about sheets and blankets for John?" Emma asked.

"Come down with me and I'll give you what's needed. You, John, can fetch water from downstairs. Take that chamber pot in Emma's room along and empty it in the privy at the back of the yard."

After making the bed, Emma unpacked the small bundle that held her possessions and John's. Besides a few spare pieces of underclothing there was only the Bible that Granny Wilbur had bequeathed to her and the tinderbox that had belonged to her father and that she had found in the ruins of the house after the fire. The Bible and the tinderbox were two legacies reminding her that the people she had loved best were dead and that she and John must now make their own way as well as they could by themselves. Mrs. McPhail was legally their guardian but she was a stranger; Emma could not imagine going to her for help or advice if she could avoid it. Not until they were twenty-one – seven years in the future for

Emma and more than nine for John – would they be free of
her and inherit the small legacies that were their share of the
proceeds from the sale of the farm.

When Emma was in bed, she reflected that the day had
seemed interminably long. This morning she had got up from
the women's communal bed in that roadside inn. Now here
she was in a different bed in York, with a much clearer –
though also grimmer – picture of what the next months or
years would be like.

    During the last few days, since making her decision to
come to York with Mrs. McPhail instead of staying in the settlement and, a year from now, marrying Isaac Bates, she had
imagined her life in York as one that would offer larger
prospects, more interesting friends, and the stimulus of books
and civilized surroundings. All that had been thrown into
doubt now. Though her parents' conversation and the few
books she had read had taught her something about social
classes, she had no real idea of how a chambermaid lived in
York. She longed so much for a larger and more civilized life
– a life that she was sure some people in York must enjoy –
but now she might be excluded from it completely.

    Because of her tiredness, because of discouragement at the
distance between her present existence and the one she had
dreamed of, she was suddenly on the verge of tears. Feeling
the need for reassurance, she reached up to the shelf above
her bed and touched the tinderbox, which was her link with
her parents – intelligent, good-humored, and resolute as they
had been – and with the way of life and thought that they had
tried to establish on that backwoods farm. She needed some
of that resoluteness and courage now.

She was still grappling with the tears when the door opened and a candle's glimmer appeared.

"Emma?"

It was John, in his nightshirt and on bare feet. She lifted the covers and he, after setting down the candle, climbed in under them. His wiry body was cold and she put her arms around him, remembering the night of the fire when the two of them had been taken in by the Wilburs and she had lain awake till dawn watching the glow of the fire while John slept.

Now John shivered for a moment and pressed against her but said nothing. He had always been reserved and self-contained, qualities that Emma, with her tendency to blurt things out, rather admired. But now she wondered whether she should encourage him to talk and, if so, how to do it without invading that clearly defined privacy of his.

"How did you get your candle lit again?" she asked.

"I never blew it out. I wanted to think, and I can't think in the dark."

Mrs. McPhail had warned them not to waste candles but this was no time to remind John of it. "What did you want to think about?"

"I wish I didn't have to start work for Mr. Blackwood right away tomorrow. Everything's so strange. Before I start working I'd first like to . . ." Instead of completing the sentence he twitched nervously.

Emma sensed his fears and wished that her mother or father were here to talk to him. What was the right thing to say? She began slowly. "But Mr. Blackwood isn't strange. We've known him for a week now, since he came to look at Father's . . . at our farm. And you'll enjoy working in a livery stable with the horses, just a few minutes' walk from here. Besides, tomorrow afternoon you'll come with Mrs. McPhail and me to buy clothes. That will give you a chance to look around."

He didn't answer; his body was rigid, and Emma realized that he was trying not to cry. Even as a baby he had seldom cried; that he should do so now indicated how unhappy he was. Emma felt as though she was being shown a part of his secret self, an unfamiliar and rather impressive personality that was coming into view at this very moment. Yet it was still her little brother, not quite twelve years old, whom she held while he struggled with his fears.

At last he whispered, so softly that she could hardly make out the words, "I wish Mother and Father were here."

"So do I," she said, remembering the stretchers covered with bedsheets beside which she had stood on that cold March morning while, a few yards away, the ruins of the house still smoked. "So do I. We'll have to manage this together, John. Let's talk about Mother and Father sometimes, and do what they would have wanted."

"Sometimes . . . sometimes it's as though I'm . . . I'm forgetting them already." Suddenly violent in the release of his anguish, he twisted in her arms and pushed his whole shaking body against her. Emma made soft noises and tried to conceal her own tears. She missed their parents too, but her danger – if it was one – was thinking of them too often. Over and over she remembered their words and ways, their gentle and thoughtful comments. She knew now that they had not been well suited to life at the very fringe of settlement; her father with his injured arm could not do all the necessary hard work and her mother's ways were perhaps too fine for such a life. Yet they had stayed on the farm for fifteen years and accomplished a great deal, mainly because they had had a little money and because they had brain and spirit to avoid being overcome by the hard conditions.

She could not reach the tinderbox now, but in her imagination she touched it and invoked her parents' help.

THREE

The Deal

he quarter-pie window was still pitch black when Emma woke to find Mrs. Jones, in nightgown and shawl, standing over them with a candle.

"Well, I guess two to a bed is warmer," the cook remarked. "And then, he's only a little lad."

"Is it time to get up?" Emma asked.

"Why, sure it is. I don't go around waking folks when there ain't no need to." She lit Emma's and John's candles from hers and then left.

"Come on, John, wake up."

Downstairs the kitchen was warm from the banked fire. Mrs. Jones, who was now seen to be a small, plump, mob-capped woman of close to fifty, stirred the ashes and added kindling wood to make a blaze and then gave Emma and John a slice of bread and jam each. "Breakfast ain't till later but it's hard to work on an empty stomach." She looked Emma up and down. "I see you found them aprons. That's good. I guess Mrs. McPhail told you that the big ones're for housework and the smaller ones for when you wait on table. The small ones get put in the laundry when they're the least bit dirty, but Mrs. McPhail ain't so fussy about the large ones. Don't make any more laundry than you have to. Mrs. Tubb can't spend all her time washing."

"I do the downstairs rooms before breakfast, don't I?"

"That's right. Here's the dusters and things. And don't make a lot of noise 'cause the guests are still asleep. You, John, get me a couple o' buckets o' water, there's a good lad. You don't go to Blackwood's till after breakfast and before then you can do a few things here. Joseph Tubb should be around and'll show you."

As he went out the back door, John gave Emma a small, tight smile but for the rest he seemed even more reserved than usual. Emma, remembering last night, wished that she could have helped him through this difficult day. But they would be apart all morning – and she herself, no doubt, had a daunting number of strange experiences ahead of her.

Just then Mrs. Tubb came in from the back kitchen.

"Here's Mrs. Tubb," observed the cook unnecessarily. "You two go on to the front now and get to work."

Emma followed Mrs. Tubb through the connecting door into the parlor. This was the room that she had glimpsed yesterday. It was large, with a dining area at the kitchen end and some chairs and the sofa near the fireplace.

When Emma and Mrs. Tubb entered, Mrs. McPhail was already there opening the curtains. Mrs. Tubb went straight to the fireplace and began raking out ashes, while Mrs. McPhail directed Emma to dust everywhere and sweep the floor.

When that was finished, Mrs. McPhail called her to the enormous cupboard near the dining table. It had a long working surface at a convenient height, with doors and drawers below and open shelves above.

"Come and let me show you where everything is kept in the dresser, Emma." She opened doors and pulled out drawers. "Here are the dishes, cutlery, napkins, and so forth. Practically everything the guests need will be put ready on the table before they sit down. You'll bring the dishes of food in from the kitchen. Anything that needs carving is put in front of me at the head of the table. You'll hand round what I carve. If people want wine or whiskey they pay extra – the bottles are here in the dresser." With a key from the bunch at her waist she unlocked one door in the lower part of the cupboard. "These bottles are refilled from casks in the cellar, of course."

"I haven't seen the . . . the barroom, or whatever it should be called."

"We don't have one. There are plenty of taverns for people who just want to drink. This is mainly a residential hotel. We do have people from outside dining here, usually friends of the guests."

At that moment Mrs. Delaney came in, wearing a small apron over her black dress. She said good morning to Emma and began setting the table.

Mrs. McPhail continued her instructions to Emma. "The guests breakfast at half past seven. This morning Louise will serve them but from tomorrow on that will be your work. After the guests are finished, you and the other servants will have breakfast. Now you had better do the lobby before the guests come down."

Emma dusted and swept the lobby, still not happy at the prospect of eating with the servants. But that turned out to be less of an ordeal than she had feared. The only people she had not met before were Joseph Tubb and his son Joe. The latter, seated across the table from her, stared Emma into blushing annoyance and confusion. He was a large boy, though he couldn't be more than twelve or thirteen, with a round face very much like his mother's and a plump, waistless body. His frequent unmotivated laughter, staring eyes, and sudden fits of winking and grimacing made Emma conclude that he must be a bit weak in the head.

Joseph Tubb was a small, hunched man with a pinched face. A deformed leg caused him to limp badly. He didn't say a word throughout the meal but gave Emma and John a few glances that seemed friendly enough.

After breakfast Mrs. Jones explained to John where Blackwood's livery stable was: "Just down the street a little ways – you'll see the sign from our gate."

John said nothing. Emma, suspecting that he was tense with his unexpressed fears, walked with him across the hotel yard to the gate. It was a chilly, overcast morning but at least just at the moment it was not raining. She tucked her hands under her apron to keep warm, and John turned up the collar of his coat.

When they stood at the gate, Emma found that she had nothing to say to him and didn't dare offend him by giving him a hug. So she patted the top of his head in what she hoped was a playful manner.

"I hope it goes all right, John. See you this afternoon."

He glanced up once to meet her eyes, then shoved his hands into his pockets and set off down the street.

Back in the kitchen, Emma was given further instructions by Mrs. Jones. "You'll have to be going upstairs with Mrs. Tubb to do the bedrooms," the cook said. Then, looking around as though to make sure they were not overheard, she went on, "I wanted to say don't mind about the Tubbs. Mrs. McPhail took 'em on 'cause they was having a hard time finding work. O'course she pays 'em less than clever people – not that Joseph ain't clever enough for most ordinary things. But when you're working with Mrs. Tubb, keep an eye on her. She sometimes goes off into a sort of staring." Mrs. Jones tried to imitate a look of goggle-eyed vacancy. "Then you have to remind her what she's supposed to be doing. There ain't no cause to be afeared of 'em."

"Joe made me . . . rather uncomfortable at breakfast," Emma admitted.

"I know, he always does that with new people. But you'll see, he'll not notice you from now on."

Then Mrs. Tubb returned, apparently from the privy because she was still adjusting the back of her dress, and she and Emma went upstairs with water for cleaning and an empty bucket for the contents of the chamber pots.

As they reached the upstairs hall, Emma heard Major Heatherington's voice. ". . . farm that Blackwood mentioned. Now that he is back I must speak with him. I didn't have the opportunity after dinner yesterday evening."

Mrs. Heatherington said something of which only the word "legacy" was discernible, and then the door opened and out came the girl whom Emma had seen on the previous afternoon. She was rather plump and very pretty, with blonde hair in artless-looking curls. But her face had a sulky, discontented expression that detracted from her charm. Still standing in the doorway, she pulled a cloak around her shoulders and fastened it at the throat.

"I don't think you need me here for your discussion of that boring old farm, Father, so I'll go and visit Mrs. Milford." She spoke in a pert voice that Emma could not imagine having used to her own parents.

"Before you go, Caroline," came the Major's voice, "please to remember that if you do not marry Captain Dixon you will have to come with us – to this farm of Blackwood's or to another one. So it would be wise either to interest yourself in the farm or to make peace with Dixon."

Without a further word, Miss Heatherington closed the door and walked down the stairs, flouncing her skirts and ignoring Emma and Mrs. Tubb.

Mrs. Tubb stared incuriously at the door of the Heatheringtons' room until Emma, remembering what Mrs. Jones had said, remarked, "I suppose we'd better begin with one of the empty rooms?"

Mrs. Tubb nodded and knocked at the door of Room One. When there was no answer she went in and began emptying the chamber pot and the washbasin into the bucket.

It appeared that Mrs. Tubb's only responsibility upstairs was seeing to the fireplaces and carrying wood, water, and slops, though she did say something about washing and waxing the floors "when it was time." Evidently such major chores were not scheduled for today. By the time Mrs. Tubb

had finished the smaller, daily work and disappeared downstairs, the Heatheringtons had gone out. Emma was left alone
on the bedroom floor of the hotel.

Before she had gone very far in the work, she recognized
the difference between overnight and longer-term guests.
The rooms of the former were just rooms, like the one she
had cleaned the previous afternoon. Those of longer-term
residents had personality. Room One was evidently occupied
by a lady who painted in watercolors and enjoyed reading and
embroidery. Besides paints and books (over which Emma
gloated for a few moments) there was a piece of fine needle-
work, and on the table by the window a small, well-equipped
portable desk was set up.

In Major and Mrs. Heatherington's room there were signs
of different tastes and personalities. On the mantelpiece were
some portraits of fashionably dressed people, a book about
travels in Upper Canada, a program from a musical evening
at Government House dated the previous Friday, and a Book
of Common Prayer. Mrs. Heatherington's sewing basket
stood beside one chair and a tray with glasses and bottles of
madeira and whiskey on a table near another one.

Connecting with that room was the one that Miss
Heatherington occupied. When Emma opened the door, she
stood still and stared. She had never in her life seen such a
profusion of clothes. Half a dozen pairs of shoes lay scattered
on the floor among petticoats and lacy pantaloons and stock-
ings. Gowns of colorful and delicate fabrics were draped over
the bed and, as Emma watched, something silky slid off the
edge to the floor. A crimson shawl was flung beautifully but
carelessly over a chair. A chest against the wall stood open to
reveal even more profusion and luxury.

Did she never tidy her belongings? Or had she tried on and rejected all these garments this morning? Had she always had the services of a lady's maid till now?

But Emma's wonder and censure melted in the presence of such loveliness. She could have knelt and gathered it all up with rapture. Then her common sense told her that she would *have* to gather it up – with or without rapture – because in the room's present state she would hardly be able to move a step without treading on something. She was wondering where to begin when Mrs. McPhail arrived to check on her progress.

"Hang the clothes on the pegs and put the shoes and boots in a row against the wall. You aren't her personal maid, so you need not do more than that, but you must clear the things away so that you can do the room. Is this your last one?"

"No, I have to do Mr. Walker's still."

"You'll become quicker with practice."

Emma was making the last bed when she felt hands seizing her hips. She whirled around and found herself facing a young gentleman with blond hair.

"Well, well, my girl," he said with a grin. "It's one pretty housemaid after another in this hotel. Where does Lady McPhail find you all?"

She turned away sharply and resumed her bedmaking.

"Not even a smile and a kiss? Come, come, madam, that's not at all friendly of you."

"I have no wish to be unfriendly, sir, but I have my job to do." She blushed at the indignity and tried to hide her fury. "I'm new here and . . ."

"Then I'll have to be the one to make you welcome, eh?" He took hold of her again.

As Emma tried to extricate herself, a lady passed the open door and paused, "Has the rain driven you back too, Mr. Tufts?" she asked, "I've just returned for my umbrella."

Emma looked at her with relief.

The lady smiled at her, "It would be as well to let the housemaid do her work, Mr. Tufts," she said pleasantly. "And I'd be glad of a word with you. You have been in York before and I wonder if you could give me some advice."

Reluctantly, he joined her in the hall and together they went down the stairs. Emma, trembling with anger, hurried to finish the room.

That afternoon, Emma and Mrs. McPhail set out for town. Emma was in good spirits, eager to see something of York. The morning's rain had stopped and the clouds were racing across the sky. Of course the ground was dreadfully muddy, but Mrs. McPhail led the way along a slightly more solid strip of road close to the fences that bordered the yards and gardens in this northern part of the town. Emma followed. Dead leaves and drops of water fell on her from the over-hanging trees but she was so interested in her surroundings that she barely noticed them. The area was clearly town rather than country but was still different from the unbroken rows of buildings that Emma had glimpsed in the center of town the day before.

She examined the houses and gardens that they passed, glancing at the laundry that a housewife had just hung on a line and watching another woman in a kerchief and man's coat briskly splitting firewood. She smiled at a girl leading a reluctant cow. She dodged the lifted tail of a horse tethered to a veranda railing.

In a few moments they reached Blackwood's livery stable, identified by a sign bearing the name and depicting a carriage pulled by a high-stepping horse.

"I will go indoors to fetch Mr. Blackwood," said Mrs. McPhail. "You could go and see if John is in the yard."

"Yes, Mrs. McPhail. Could I ask what that smell is? I don't recognize it."

Mrs. McPhail lifted her rather handsome face and sniffed. "That's the brewery and the tannery. Actually it's not very strong today. Some of my guests complain when the wind blows it straight toward the hotel."

"Thank you. I'll go and look for John."

But just then John and Mr. Blackwood appeared from the wide entrance to the stable yard. Mr. Blackwood greeted Emma and Mrs. McPhail with a raised hat and gave his arm to the latter. Majestically they led the way toward town.

"How did everything go this morning?" Emma asked John as they walked along a short distance behind their elders.

He gave her a glance in which there was no sign of last night's fear. In fact, it was a distinctly cool glance, and for a moment Emma was hurt, until she recognized that John was probably using coolness to protect himself.

"Fine. I helped muck out the barn and held horses for customers. I work with an old fellow called Fred who's all right."

"And Mr. Blackwood?" Emma whispered, looking at the broad figure ahead of them.

John shrugged. "I guess I won't be seeing much of him."

No, thought Emma, *just as I probably won't be seeing as much of Mrs. McPhail as of Mrs. Jones.*

Ahead of them, visible between two buildings at the foot of Yonge Street, was the lake with its distant fringe of peninsula and islands encircling the harbor. Emma remembered her father drawing a map of the area, showing where the fort was and the roads leading east and west to other towns and the world beyond. As she gazed at the visible bit of lake, a boat with a brown sail crossed it and her heart lifted anew.

Their first stop was the office where sales and purchases of land were registered. The clerk checked his records and discovered that Martin Anderson had indeed taken up two hundred acres of land in Flamborough Township, about five miles from the village of Waterdown, in 1814. Now that farm was to be sold to Mr. Jeremiah Blackwood.

Emma's presence on this occasion was the result of a talk she had had with Mrs. McPhail before the trip to York. Emma had been suspicious of this aunt who had suddenly appeared in time to claim an inheritance from her deceased half-brother. Neither she nor John had ever seen her before – and besides, Mrs. McPhail was so reluctant to talk about herself that even good-natured Mr. Wilbur had been uneasy.

Mr. Jameson, the lawyer who had made Martin Anderson's will and whom Emma had visited in Dundas, had confirmed that Mrs. McPhail really was Martin Anderson's half-sister and therefore Emma's aunt, but Emma still feared some dishonest dealing, especially when the only person interested in buying the farm was a friend of Mrs. McPhail's. So she had asked to be present when the sale of the farm was registered, the proceeds were divided according to the terms of her father's will, and her inheritance and John's were put in the bank.

The clerk was making out a deed of sale. "Purchase price is three hundred dollars, I believe you said, sir?" he asked, looking up at Mr. Blackwood.

"Yes."

"Is that a reasonable price?" Emma asked the clerk.

The clerk looked surprised at her speaking out but he answered readily enough. "Yes, not bad. It's a remote location, no lake or river frontage, that sort of thing. Your aunt is lucky to have found a buyer so soon. Plenty of abandoned farms lie empty for years and benefit nobody."

Emma was hurt at hearing her home called an abandoned farm but she acknowledged that the clerk was probably right.

Mr. Blackwood paid the money to Mrs. McPhail and then left them; the others went to the Bank of Upper Canada where, under the banker's eye, the money was divided. Mrs. McPhail received seventy-five dollars and Emma and John one hundred and twelve dollars and fifty cents each. The banker arranged all the details of the trust into which their shares were put. He too was surprised at Emma's interest.

"You realize, young lady, that you and your brother can't touch this until each of you is twenty-one. Then the trust will be wound up and you will be able to use the money as you wish."

"Can Mrs. McPhail take it out? As our guardian?"

"No. No one can."

Emma knew that she ought to be content with all these assurances, but she was still uneasy. She watched Mrs. McPhail dip the pen and sign one of the documents. Was there a hint of smugness in the smooth face under the dignified black hat? When Mrs. McPhail had first appeared in their lives, two weeks ago, Emma had wondered why a lady like her should be apparently pleased at having become the guardian of a niece and nephew who might very well be a nuisance to her. That question had been answered when it became obvious that Mrs. McPhail would inherit something under the will and that Emma and John could be put to work.

Perhaps Mrs. McPhail's present smugness was simply the result of satisfaction at selling the farm. All the same, when they left the bank Emma did not feel completely sure that everything had been done in a fair and honorable way. But there was no one stage of the transactions on which to focus her unease.

FOUR

Doors Opening

W hen Emma returned to her room later that afternoon, she dropped her bundles and sat down on the bed with a sigh. She had never before in her life had such an afternoon of shopping and trying on clothes and just *seeing things*. The sheer abundance of merchandise had awed and excited her. In her mind's eye she still saw bolts of fabric stacked almost to the ceiling, in every imaginable color, luxurious fabrics as well as utilitarian ones. She had seen lace and gloves and hats and shawls, delicate dancing slippers, fur muffs, and fans.

Oddly enough, the knowledge that such wonders existed had even reconciled her to the two black dresses that had been bought for her. They were the best clothes she had ever owned, and she had vowed that they would be only the beginning of a

43

new wardrobe. Of course on her wages of two dollars per month she could not afford clothes immediately but she could think and dream. The well-dressed women whom she had seen on the street and in the shops had given her something to dream about.

The pleasurable sigh was not only for the clothes. She had seen a bookstore and intended to return to it when she was in town alone. She had liked the straight, wide streets full of activity. She enjoyed the immense variety of people, sober and flamboyant, elegant and dowdy. John had spotted a black man whom Mrs. McPhail had identified as a hotel owner named Mr. Snow, which John had at first thought must be a joke but that was actually his name. Two ladies in the clothing store had spoken a foreign language that, again according to Mrs. McPhail, was German. It was very exciting.

Perhaps the biggest surprise of the afternoon had to do with Mrs. McPhail. For the first time since Emma had met her, she had softened a bit. She seemed willing to answer questions and had in some subtle way treated Emma like a niece rather than an employee. On the way back to the hotel she had walked with Emma and John rather than ahead of them. When they reached Blackwood's and John was about to go into the stable yard, she said that he need not return to work. "I've arranged with Mr. Blackwood that you may have the rest of the afternoon off." And even John's being put to work in the hotel garden after that did not quite spoil the effect.

But now, back in the hotel, Emma was the chambermaid again. She had to wash and change into one of the new dresses and then go downstairs to help prepare dinner.

Knowing that she still had a few minutes of free time, she went to the quarter-pie window to see what sort of view there was. This was really the first time she'd been in the room by daylight.

The window faced north and, being in the attic of a tall house, looked over the nearby roofs toward farms and a low wooded ridge beyond. In the immediate foreground was the hotel's yard and garden, where Joseph and John were pulling carrots. At the hotel's gate stood a brewer's dray from which a keg of beer was unloaded and carried into the kitchen on the carter's shoulder.

Emma felt rich. The town was there for her to explore. Here in front of her was a beautiful scene, more civilized than the surroundings in which she had grown up and brilliant with autumn colors. Her heart responded to the beauty. What glory, to live in such a varied and interesting world! Even a chambermaid could enjoy it.

Down in the garden, John laughed at something Joseph said, and the carter whistled as he walked back to his wagon. Emma, with another happy sigh, turned away from the window.

When she had the dress on, she looked at herself in the tiny mirror and recalled what she had seen in the full-length mirror in the shop. The dress was V-necked and had sleeves coming to just below the elbow. The black was slightly relieved by the white kerchief draped over her shoulders and tucked into the neckline in front. She still disliked having to wear black but admitted that it set off her fine-textured red-head's skin and the hair that, though not red, was the bur-nished, glinting brown of acorns. Using the pins that Mrs. McPhail had bought her, she subdued the fluff of unruly hair about her face and tried to gather it all into the single long braid down her back. But the slicked-back style looked wrong and in the end she left the fluff as it had always been.

45

Before going downstairs she put on the new low boots. They were rather stiff and she hoped they wouldn't give her blisters but they fitted better than any other pair she had tried on in the store.

It took all her awareness of being well dressed to give her the courage to appear before the guests in her guise as waitress. The afternoon's happiness and liberation were over; she was so nervous and tense that she had hardly any room left over for resenting the apron.

But after all, the work was not as difficult and unpleasant as Emma had feared. Mrs. Heatherington smiled at her and Mr. Blackwood greeted her in his big voice but no one else paid any attention.

Mrs. McPhail sat at one end of the table with Mr. Blackwood beside her. Opposite him was the lady who had rescued Emma from the persistent young man that morning and whose name was Miss Morgan. She was perhaps thirty years old, with dark brown hair in a loose bun and a rather forthright manner.

The Heatheringtons were grouped at the other end; with them was a young man in the red coat of an army officer, soon identified as the Captain Dixon whom Major Heatherington had mentioned that morning. Along the table between these parties sat two or three solitary people.

As the meal progressed, Emma began to notice what went on among the guests. She was not busy all the time; during the lulls when nothing was required of her she stood beside the dresser, watching and listening. She was especially interested in the Heatherington party. Captain Dixon glanced often at Miss Heatherington, who was wearing a pale green gown with a low neckline and enormous puffed sleeves.

When he spoke to her she answered rather curtly but she did occasionally look at him assessingly when he was talking to someone else.

He talked mostly with Mrs. Heatherington, and Emma gathered that they shared friends or relatives in England. "You must know the Turners too," he said to Caroline Heatherington at one point, "because they are close neighbors of your aunt and uncle in Sussex and visit them often." This gave Emma a tantalizing glimpse of English country houses and elegant ladies strolling across lawns. She dwelled on it until Mrs. McPhail beckoned her to hand around the platter of carved roast again.

When Emma was once more at leisure, Major Heatherington was telling a story about something that had happened to him in Gibraltar. "So in the end we had to learn some Spanish after all," he concluded, and Captain Dixon asked Mrs. Heatherington if she had had to speak Spanish to the servants. This gave Emma another mental picture and probably explained why the Major and his wife looked so sun-browned. Curiously, their daughter did not fit into that picture at all.

After the meal, when the guests had taken their cups of tea or coffee to the sofa and chairs at the other end of the room or gone out, and when Emma had finished clearing the table, Mrs. McPhail asked her to come to her own room for a moment.

Mrs. McPhail sat down at the desk and gestured Emma to the chair beside it.

"I wanted to tell you first of all that Mrs. Delaney is no longer in service here. She took my place while I was away to settle the matter of you and John and the farm, and I would have considered giving her work for a little longer – she is an acquaintance of mine from Boston and has some hotel experience – but she did not suit. Mrs. Jones disliked her and I consider it to be her fault that Sally, your predecessor, left. I am telling you this because I gather Mrs. Delaney intends to stay in York for a while and you may meet her." Mrs. McPhail smiled thinly. "If she tries to enlist your sympathies against me, I trust you will know whom to believe."

"Yes, Mrs. McPhail."

"And one other thing. You are good at simple sewing. Mrs. Jones has some linen that needs mending. Please attend to that during the coming days, in the afternoons. For work of that sort, of course, you will sit in the kitchen where it is warm, not in your bedroom. In fact, the kitchen is where you will spend any free time that you do not use for exercise or errands outside the hotel."

"Yes, ma'am," Emma said, while telling herself that, whatever the instructions, she would sit in her room when she needed privacy more than warmth. She had spotted a small wooden armchair among the old furniture in the attic and had wondered about moving that into her room.

"I may say, Emma, that I am pleased with your work and general deportment so far. If you continue as you have started you will do well enough." She nodded dismissal. "That will be all, then."

"If I may ask one question, ma'am? . . ."

Mrs. McPhail's eyebrows lifted very slightly. "Yes?"

"Now that I am in York I would like to find out a bit more about my parents. They both lived here before moving to the farm and I thought there might be old friends of theirs to whom I could talk. Do you know of anyone?"

"I don't believe there is anyone," Mrs. McPhail said decidedly. "Your father, of course, joined the army and was wounded at the battle of Queenston Heights; the troops stationed at the fort are changed fairly frequently and there is certainly no one there now who served with him."

"He must have had friends outside the army."

Mrs. McPhail shrugged. "I know of no one. And I have no information at all about your mother, whom I never met."

Emma knew that a door had been closed in her face but she was not sure what, if anything, there was beyond that door. Mrs. McPhail might indeed not know of anyone who could give information about Martin and Anne Anderson. Emma was very well aware that the Andersons had not been on especially friendly terms with her. On the other hand, something in Mrs. McPhail's manner made Emma wonder. She would try elsewhere, though at this moment she had no idea where to begin.

"Thank you, ma'am," she said, as though satisfied with Mrs. McPhail's answer. "Good night."

"Good night, Emma."

As Emma reached for the doorknob, there was a knock.

"That will be Mr. Blackwood," said Mrs. McPhail. "You may let him in."

Mr. Blackwood came in, greeting Mrs. McPhail and wishing Emma good night. As Emma closed the door behind her, she heard him say to Mrs. McPhail, "*That* deal went through very well, I thought. Now for . . ."

Tired after the long day, Emma fetched her candle and jug of water from the kitchen and went up the stairs.

Not until she was halfway up the last flight did the significance of Mr. Blackwood's words strike her. She stopped in her tracks. What exactly had he said? "That deal went through very well. Now for . . ." Could he be talking about his purchase of the Anderson farm today – purchased from Mrs. McPhail who was executrix of Martin Anderson's will? And could the last two words mean that he and Mrs. McPhail were going to discuss the next step?

And this morning she had overheard Major Heatherington refer to "this farm of Blackwood's" to which he and his wife might be moving – and Caroline too if she did not marry Captain Dixon.

The Heatheringtons were thinking of buying her old home!

But perhaps Blackwood had other farms to sell. Sobered by that thought, Emma went up the last few steps and into her room. Was it even remotely likely that the Heatheringtons – well-traveled, sophisticated people – would buy and live on the old Anderson farm, two days' journey from York in a frontier hamlet so new and small that it didn't even have a name yet, a farm with only a few acres cleared, a burned-out ruin of a house, a barn, and a tiny one-room shanty?

Of course it was a good shanty, with a window and a wooden floor and a proper fireplace. Martin and Anne Anderson, with the baby Emma after she was born, had lived there for five years until the house was built. It was almost possible to imagine Major and Mrs. Heatherington there; if they had lived in military garrisons they must be used to simple lodgings.

Oh, if only they did buy it! She flung her arms wide in delight and was about to do a little dance of joy when she heard Mrs. Jones cross the attic and go into the room next door. So she had to be joyful in silence.

As the elation simmered down a bit she went to the quarter-pie window and leaned her forehead against the cool, black glass. Knowing that the Heatheringtons were living on the beloved farm would be the next best thing to having her parents brought back to life. Perhaps in some way she could manage to go and visit them, see the farm and the neighbors again, stand beside the wild grape vines on the hill and the dark stream among the cedar trees, watch the swallows scooping in and out of the barn. With the Heatheringtons there, it would still in some way be home.

FIVE

The New Life

In the next few days, Emma's new life took shape. She came to know and like Mrs. Jones, who could be gruff when she was busy, and who bargained keenly with the peddlers who came to the door selling everything from fish to baskets. Mrs. Jones had to account for every penny spent in the kitchen; each evening she spread out her account book on the kitchen table, fetched her ink and pen from the dresser and, with much frowning and chewing the soft end of the quill and great effort to make her writing legible, wrote down what she had bought that day and how much she had paid for it. Then she would say "That's *that*" with emphatic relief and make herself a cup of tea to drink while she sat knitting by the fire.

During the afternoons, while mending the linen, Emma watched with irritated pity as Mrs. Tubb struggled with the hotel's more disagreeable work – cleaning the remnants of wax out of candlesticks, polishing brass and silver, laundering and ironing, carrying ashes, wood, water, and slops. Some of the carrying should actually have been done by her son but he was not there nearly as often as he was needed, and neither Mrs. Tubb nor anyone else seemed able to make him do more than he wanted to do.

Emma's own routine took very much the shape that Mrs. McPhail had outlined on that first evening. She was busy the whole of every day, from soon after rising at five o'clock until about half past nine in the evening, when she went to bed.

On Friday, in addition to her regular work, she had to do Mrs. McPhail's rooms. "Only sweeping and dusting," Mrs. McPhail said. "I make the bed myself and Mrs. Tubb does the heavy work. Oh, and please fill the whale-oil lamp whenever necessary." She pointed to the lamp standing on the desk. "Mrs. Jones will show you where the oil is kept."

Emma had been surprised that her aunt, who was so very reserved and protective of her privacy, should let anyone see her bedroom. Tantalized by that reserve, she looked forward to what she might discover. She was sure that bedrooms revealed a great deal about the personalities of their occupants – look at the guests' rooms upstairs!

In her heart of hearts she hoped to learn something important, though she had no idea what it might be.

Mrs. McPhail's sitting room she had already seen; the only new information she gleaned this time was that the writing desk had several drawers in it. She was tempted to try whether they were locked but didn't; her mother had taught her to respect other people's belongings and Emma hated the thought of prying.

The bedroom beyond was almost as unrevealing as the sitting room. There were a comb and hairbrush on a shelf under a mirror and, hanging on the walls, reproductions of two portraits – of Queen Elizabeth and Queen Anne, according to a little painted scroll on each. A clothes chest stood in a corner with a folded black shawl lying on top and two pairs of sturdy low boots standing next to it. The bedside table was covered by a beautifully embroidered cloth – probably Mrs. McPhail's own work – on which a small Bible lay. On the floor beside the bed was a braided rug. At the windows hung heavy dark blue curtains. Both rooms, because they were already so tidy, were easy to dust and sweep.

Emma's first reaction was that she had learned nothing new about her aunt. The choice of pictures was suggestive – was Mrs. McPhail interested in English monarchs, or did she like to see herself as queen of her own little domain? – and so was the neatness and the absence of trivial objects. Emma, although inexperienced in such things, was sure that everything was of good quality; certainly the mirror gave the clearest reflection she had ever seen and the curtains were made of rich-feeling fabric. Although it was hard to define, she somehow felt that she knew her aunt a little better now.

On Saturday Emma was awakened, even before Mrs. Jones called her, by a strange mixture of farmyard noises and the shouting of men, which came in bursts from the street. There were also flickering lights showing against her ceiling. At breakfast she asked Mrs. Jones about it.

"Farmers goin' to market, lass. Them noises are from the cows and pigs they bring in to sell."

Immediately after breakfast, Mrs. Jones herself set off for the market, accompanied by young Joe carrying two huge baskets.

The Sunday routine was only slightly different from that of the weekdays. The servants were allowed to sleep until half past five because the guests breakfasted half an hour later than usual. But all the rooms had to be swept and all the beds made.

In the afternoon Mrs. McPhail took her niece and nephew to church. Emma looked forward to the occasion, not because she was religious but because it was another new experience. She had never been to church – neither the settlement nor Waterdown had a church, though the latter was served by itinerant preachers at intervals – but her parents had always, every Sunday, arranged for a quiet hour of prayer and Bible reading and discussion.

She was impressed by the appearance of St. James' Church as they approached it, but all her pleasure was spoiled when she learned that she and John would have to stand in the back with the other servants and poor people. The pews were reserved for those who rented them; Mrs. McPhail sat with friends in their pew.

"Do we have to come every Sunday?" John whispered.

"I'll have to ask. I hope not."

Without a hymn book or prayer book she was unable to follow the proceedings very well. The sermon was a discourse on some obscure passage in the Bible combined with a high-minded but, Emma thought, basically uninteresting admonition to everyone to do his or her duty. Only the music, which was provided by a small military band, excited and delighted her.

Mrs. McPhail had told Emma and John that after the service they would return to the hotel by themselves. Taking this to mean that they need not hurry, they lingered outside the church to watch the congregation leave. They overheard someone saying that the most fashionable people went to the morning service, but even so there were half a dozen handsome carriages waiting in the street and a number of well-dressed families standing and talking in the heavily overcast October afternoon. Several army officers in red coats were present and other people in the whole range from sober luxury to threadbareness. Some beggars were about, trying to avoid notice while hoping for charity. Children, temporarily free from restraint, ran in and out among the adults.

Mrs. McPhail walked off with the lady and gentleman whose pew she had shared.

A moment later it began to rain. Several umbrellas appeared and the crowd dispersed rapidly. Emma and John, though they would have been happy to do something special on this free afternoon, could think of nowhere to go in the rain so they returned to the hotel.

Mrs. Jones was dozing by the kitchen fire. When their arrival wakened her, she suggested tea and buttered toast, which consoled them for the wet weather and the disappointing church service.

On the following Tuesday, Mrs. McPhail asked Emma to go to Mr. Quettin St. George's store – the one where they had bought Emma's dresses – for some flannelette, buttons, and thread. This was the first time Emma had been out in town alone and she meant to enjoy it.

Almost as soon as she left the hotel she could see the lake, and this time she decided to inspect it from near by. It glittered and danced in the bright autumn afternoon. As Emma walked along with her eyes on the vista, a boat with a white sail crossed the space between the buildings at the end of the street.

But when she stood beside it, the lake was another matter. In the distance it still glittered but here by the shore it merely sloshed against the slimy pile of a wharf and over a stretch of muddy beach, lifting and shifting a revolting scum of dead fish and vegetable garbage, bits of blackened wood, old boots, and other filth. A small rowboat with a broken bow lay on the mud, and a skinny dog was rooting among the piles. Someone shouted, but not at her. Shivering in the shadow of a building on the wharf, she stared out to where the water still sparkled. A canoe was visible off to the right, and the boat she had seen earlier was still moving westward to the entrance of the harbor. She wondered whether the water out there was as dirty as it was here. Then, a little less buoyant in mood and step, she turned and walked back to King Street, where most of the stores were.

Once there, she made slow progress. There was considerable traffic of horsemen, carriages, wagons, and pedestrians. The flow was held up by a wagon that had lost a wheel and most of its load of sawn lumber. At another spot a carriage stood still in the middle of the street while the lady inside spoke to an officer. Walking close to the buildings so that she could look in at the shop windows, Emma nearly tripped over a ragged man sleeping on the ground and snoring hoarsely.

At Mr. Quettin St. George's store – which, according to Mrs. Jones, was now actually Mr. Baldwin's – she carefully matched the fabric, buttons, and thread for her aunt.

"Please put it on Mrs. Harriet McPhail's account," she said to the young man as he was tying string around her parcel. That was what Mrs. McPhail had told her to say.

For a moment the young man looked doubtful; he went away and had a whispered conference with a person barely visible at the back of the store. When he returned, he asked, "Are you the young lady who was here with Mrs. McPhail last week?"

"Yes. I'm her niece." This was no time to be merely the servant.

"That will be fine, then, miss. I'll put it on the account."

When she was outside again she crossed the street to look at the books displayed in Mr. Lesslie's store window. Several stood upright between two bookends. At that distance Emma could not read the titles, which were in tiny gold print on the brown and dark red spines, but she could conjure up whole shelves of their counterparts, row on row to the ceiling. Even more important, she could imagine the compact weight of a book in her hand, the thrill of opening it.

Closer by, one book lay open. It was much larger than the ones standing upright and was open at a page headed "Chapter Seven: Rome" and a picture of a white domed building. She had nearly finished reading the page of text, which was a glowing description of the beauties of Rome, when a running urchin crashed into her and nearly knocked her down. After she recovered her balance, she read the last few lines and then turned to go home. She hoped that when she next came this way Mr. Lesslie would have a different book open in the window.

Intending to take a different route back to the hotel, she turned into what seemed a convenient side street. There she found herself face to face with an unfamiliar aspect of the town, although it took her a minute to figure out what the strange quality was. King Street had been busy and prosperous, filled with carriages and wagons and shoppers, gentry and working people in orderly and purposeful activity. Here there was none of that. It wasn't exactly a slum, so far as Emma could tell, but people were idling about and there was no visible work going on. Girls and women leaned in doorways and over window sills, and some men hung about in front of a tavern from which came noisy talk and laughter. A girl of about eight stared at Emma in a very discomfiting way.

Suddenly two young women stepped out of a doorway and blocked her path.

"Just . . . visiting, ducky?" asked one of them.

"Or prospecting?" said the other with a laugh.

Emma was bewildered. "No, I don't know anyone here to visit. I'm on my way home. I'm a stranger."

They looked her up and down. One of them was smiling and the other was examining her with wide-eyed interest, which might have been kindly but which all the same Emma distrusted.

She would have stepped around them and walked on but, looking about, she saw that several other people were watching the scene. Suddenly she was very frightened. She didn't know what she had blundered into but she didn't like it. And she was sure that she should try not to show her fear.

"What trade are you in, dear?" one of the girls asked.

Emma had heard about wellborn girls who were kidnapped and held for ransom. Wouldn't it be better to claim humble status?

"I . . . I'm a chambermaid . . . in a hotel."

"A chambermaid!" the girl repeated with a hoot of laughter. "Whaddaya know about that!"

"We're chambermaids too, sort of," said the other one, appearing to address Emma in friendly confidence. "I guess you might call us that."

A tall man in a wide-brimmed hat came lounging out of the tavern. He plunged his hands into his pockets, rocked back on his heels, and appraised Emma. He was sufficiently well dressed so that at first, in her desperate need for help, she took him for a gentleman. But the bold look in his eyes quenched the appeal that she had been about to make.

"How nice," he said, "to see a lovely lady like you in our midst." His voice had a caressing quality.

"She's a chambermaid – so she *says*," the noisy girl informed him with a laugh. Several of the watchers, who had been silently moving closer, giggled and sniggered.

Emma blushed furiously; the man's words seemed polite, even complimentary, but she knew perfectly well that she was being mocked and insulted. Also she was becoming more frightened than ever by those people quietly closing in – women in shawls, dirty children, a boy with pale eyes and a sagging chin who stared at her with horrible fixity.

The other girl opened her eyes wide and spoke to the man. "She also said she was a stranger here in Henrietta Street. I think we should be friendly to her, don't you?"

"You mean take her in, make her one of the family . . . that sort of thing? A very good thought, girls – just like your usual kindness." As he spoke, his eyes stayed on Emma.

She had to get out of here! And she would have to go back the way she had come because by now the crowd nearly blocked the street. She turned and, gathering up her skirts,

ran. At any moment they might grab her from behind. A
ragged wave of laughter followed her, led by the hooting of
the noisy girl. Out of the corner of her eye she caught a
movement; something flew across the street ahead of her and
a dog ran after it. She swerved and stumbled but, except for
the dog, the street was clear and she ran on.

Just as she reached King Street she heard her name called.

"Emma! Hello, there! What's the matter?"

She glanced wildly around, looking for the new danger, but
it was only Mrs. Delaney, surveying Emma with her head
slightly tilted in question. Emma was glad to see her but too
agitated to speak.

"Heavens, dearie, you're all in a tremble!"

"Yes . . . ," faltered Emma. She glanced back at Henrietta
Street; the laughing crowd had almost dispersed, and closer
by the only person to be seen was a boy throwing a stick for
his dog to fetch.

"Did you stumble into Henrietta Street by accident?"

"It's . . . *wicked*! What goes on there, Mrs. Delaney? They
seemed to be all . . . in on something together. And it was as
though they hated me. How can they hate me when they
don't even know me?"

"That's where the prostitutes live, dearie."

"Prostitutes!" She knew about prostitutes from reading
Tom Jones and asking her parents to explain some puzzling
passages. But this was the first time she had encountered any.

Then her mind made a further connection. Various things
that had been said just now by the denizens of Henrietta
Street suddenly made sense. When she remembered the
remarks about chambermaids she blushed again. "Oh, no!
They thought . . ."

Mrs. Delaney put her hand on Emma's arm and gripped it with reassuring firmness. "Never mind, they were probably just teasing you. Who cares what they think?" She looked curiously at Emma. "Didn't Mrs. McPhail warn you about Henrietta Street?"

"No, she never mentioned it. She didn't warn me about anything."

"I guess she ain't got much maternal instinct," said Mrs. Delaney. "I don't suppose there's any need to warn you not to go there again."

In all the agitation, Emma had lost her sense of direction and had been slowly walking along with Mrs. Delaney. But now that she was safe, she felt herself trembling and would dearly have liked to sit down, preferably at home in her own room or in Mrs. Jones' comfortable kitchen. She was about to ask Mrs. Delaney to direct her back to the hotel when Mrs. Delaney's hand again gripped Emma's arm and pulled her to a standstill. "Shhh. Look over there!"

She pointed across the street and Emma saw Caroline Heatherington, her hand tucked into the arm of a tall, slender man in a red coat. As they watched, she laughed up at him and then appeared to press herself against him for a moment.

"Miss Heatherington! But that's not Captain Dixon."

"No, that there's Captain Marshall," said Mrs. Delaney with a significant look at Emma.

"But I thought . . ." Emma began, but she stopped for fear of saying something foolish.

"Major and Mrs. Heatherington're a bit too trusting, in my opinion," said Mrs. Delaney confidingly.

"But I heard Major Heatherington speak quite firmly to his daughter."

"They both *talk* firm sometimes, but they leave her go her own way. She tells them she's with the wife of one of the officers and they never check up."

"Goodness me!"

Mrs. Delaney cocked her head and adopted a thoughtful look, which to Emma seemed artificial. "I sometimes think it's all because they didn't bring her up themselves."

"What do you mean?" asked Emma as she was clearly expected to do.

"Well, you know her father was in the army and was stationed in some very peculiar places."

"Such as Gibraltar."

"Yes. Well, it seems that Mrs. Heatherington generally went with him."

"I think that's a very nice and . . . and wifely thing for her to do."

"Oh, sure. But you see, English children whose parents're abroad are always sent back to England to live. India and Gibraltar and places like that ain't considered healthy for children. Mrs. Heatherington could've chosen to go back to England with Caroline. Make a home for her there."

"Oh, I see." Emma recognized the difficult decision that Mrs. Heatherington must have had to make.

"Instead Caroline was sent to live with an aunt and uncle. For years I don't suppose she saw her parents much – maybe didn't see 'em at all."

Emma didn't need to ask how Mrs. Delaney had learned all this; she had seen enough of life in the hotel to know that guests often talked as though the servants were absent or deaf.

"No wonder she doesn't seem . . . related to them. Why is she with them now, though?"

"I guess they had to take charge of her again sooner or later."

"Why are they here?"

"He's retired from the army. Officers go on half pay after they retire. Quite a lot of 'em have been coming here lately because in England they can't live like gentry on half pay."

"So the Heatheringtons aren't very rich?"

Mrs. Delaney laughed. "They're richer'n you and me, dearie, but they're not very rich compared to other gentlefolk."

"Then how is it that Caroline has such expensive clothes?"

"Bought by her aunt and uncle, maybe. From what I heard, she lived with them until just before she'n her parents left England."

While talking, they had been walking slowly along King Street and had turned off into a side street.

"This is Church Street," said Mrs. Delaney with another laugh. "You ought to be pretty safe on Church Street. And here's where I'm living now. The Anchor."

They had stopped in front of an unpretentious and slightly rundown tavern with a swinging sign depicting an anchor. Beside the building was a muddy alley leading to a yard behind.

Emma's face must have registered the unflattering comparison that she was making between it and her aunt's hotel. Mrs. Delaney laughed again, "It's none so bad, girl, especially when you can't afford better. Why not come in and have a drop of something? You look like you could do with it. Are you always so pale?"

The story about the Heatheringtons had half distracted Emma but she was still shaky. She did not much care for the appearance of the Anchor but it would be good to sit down for a few minutes. So she followed Mrs. Delaney into the tavern's public room. It was a low-ceilinged, black-beamed place furnished only with one long table and its side benches. At this time of the afternoon it was nearly empty of people – the only occupants were two workmen who sat at one end of the table talking in low voices – but was filled with the smell of beer and stale tobacco smoke. The landlord was behind the bar fixing a spigot into a barrel. He looked up when Mrs. Delaney approached the bar.

"Two glasses of wine, if you please, Jack, and put it on tick."

With a glance at Emma, he filled two glasses with red wine from a handsome but not very clean decanter. Mrs. Delaney carried them to the unoccupied end of the table.

Emma was sure that she ought not be doing this but she needed to rest for a few minutes and maybe the wine would help make her feel better. So she sat down on the bench and touched her glass with a tentative finger. She was used to drinking her mother's homemade wine, diluted with water, but this was grown-up wine, seeming to suggest that Mrs. Delaney considered her an adult. Emma liked that, but all the same she glanced around the dim pub with some anxiety. She remembered Mrs. McPhail warning her against Mrs. Delaney; besides, she suspected that this was not a place for a girl to be.

"I bet you like it at the hotel, eh? Lots of life. Quite a change from out there on the farm." Mrs. Delaney drank some of her wine, keeping her eyes on Emma over the edge of the glass.

Something avid in Mrs. Delaney's face made Emma reluctant to say too much. She had seen the same look a few minutes ago when Mrs. Delaney was watching Caroline

Heatherington. It was as though she was eager for information about other people's lives and affairs, and it made Emma uneasy.

"Yes, it is a change," she admitted, sipping the wine and finding it sour.

"I liked it at the hotel. Haven't found another situation yet. Do you think your aunt would take me on again?"

Emma was startled. "How do you know she's my aunt?"

"Oh, I know all about it, dearie. She hired me about a month ago, not long after I arrived in town. She needed someone to look after the hotel while she went to Dundas to see the lawyer and then to fetch you and your little brother. I had some hotel experience in Boston."

"Boston?"

"That's where I met your aunt. And Blackwood too. That was years ago. Just this last summer I fell on hard times there and come up here to see if I could find something." Her voice and face suggested dissatisfaction and she drank the remainder of her wine at a gulp. Emma took another sip of hers. The man behind the counter was watching them, probably because he had finished installing the spigot and now seemed to have nothing else to do.

"But," Mrs. Delaney went on, "you didn't tell me whether you think your aunt would take me on again."

"I'm afraid I have no idea. There doesn't seem to be a vacancy."

"A person can always make a vacancy for a friend. But your aunt is so darned businesslike that she'd have to work it all out in figures first, see if it fitted in the budget, rather than doing a favor. Favors usually ain't good business. Don't you want your wine, dearie?"

It seemed a good cue. Emma got to her feet. "Actually I really must go home now." She picked up her parcel from the table.

"Oh, well, the rest'll go back in the bottle, won't it, Jack?"

As Emma turned at the door, she saw Mrs. Delaney carrying the almost untouched glass of wine back to the bar. In a moment's fixed tableau she saw them standing there, Mrs. Delaney and the bartender, one on each side of the bar, both of them staring at her with great concentration. Something in their look made her shiver, and the door latch rattled under her hand. Not even a gesture or word of good-bye interrupted their intent gaze.

SIX

New Friends

When Emma was awakened on the Saturday of that week by farmers going to market, she listened to the sounds with more interest. Horses, sheep, and cattle were herded along, each group of animals by several men who talked and laughed. There were dogs too, whose barking could be heard occasionally. Some groups must be very small, and when there was only the sound of one set of hooves Emma imagined a man with a single cow or horse. Carts and wagons passed too, presumably laden with produce; sometimes the indignant cackle of fowl merged with the creak of wheels. All this she could discern from the sounds and from the different ways in which the lanterns or torches impressed and slid the shape of her quarter-pie window against the ceiling of the room.

She was interested in the sounds and pictures because today she was going to the market with Mrs. Jones. Mrs. McPhail had told her so yesterday evening. She would have to gobble her breakfast and, after returning from the market, do the bedrooms very quickly – "but without skimping!" Mrs. McPhail had warned.

"Am I to take over the marketing from Mrs. Jones eventually?"

"I have no such plan, but I'd like you to be able to do it when she is ill."

So it came about that, on that Saturday morning, soon after nine o'clock, Mrs. Jones and Emma set out, with Joe carrying the baskets.

"Is there a market only on Saturdays?" Emma asked.

"The shops in the market building are open on other days, but Saturday is when most of the farmers come in with the livestock and vegetables and meat. We really should've been there earlier to get the best produce, but o'course the guests had to have their breakfast."

"It's a bit of an outing, isn't it?" Emma remarked, pleased to be outdoors on a fine fall morning rather than doing the guests' bedrooms. Mrs. Jones must enjoy it too; she hardly ever went out except to the market or occasionally to the shops on King Street. Emma looked down at the round little woman with her shawl crossed and pinned at the waist and thought that there was more spring in her step than usual.

The market was a long building surrounded by open space. Along the outer walls of the building, shutters had been raised to reveal shops where cuts of meat and whole fowl hung from hooks, or dairy products were ranged in rows and baskets. The open area around the building was crowded.

Cattle and horses were being sold or traded in one corner, and some farmers were selling produce from their wagons. Geese were tethered by their feet to the fence.

Mrs. Jones exchanged greetings and news with friends, including the vendors, but in between she showed Emma how to recognize the freshness of fish by the look of the gills and eyes, the age of fowl by the length of the spurs.

"Young birds have short spurs," she said, holding a dead hen's foot and wiggling the toes. "O'course sometimes you want old fowl. But watch out for a spur that's been clipped short. Mr. Davidson here, he'd never clip a spur," she said, smiling a warning at the farmer beside the wagon, "but there's them that would."

Emma concentrated hard to try to remember it all. Fortunately when they came to the vegetables it was easier because Emma had learned a good deal about them from her mother. Anne Anderson had been brought up on a farm and had taught Emma how to grow and cook quite a variety of vegetables. Mrs. Jones, like Emma's mother, handled food carefully and knew what she was doing. They even had some of the same customs, Emma had noticed, like cutting a cross into the top of a loaf of bread before putting it into the oven to bake. "To keep off witches," Anne Anderson had explained. She always smiled as she spoke but never forgot the crosses on the bread.

When the shopping was done, Mrs. Jones and Emma paused for a minute or two near the pillory, where a man was standing with his head and hands locked into a wooden frame. He was not at all abashed by the punishment but was shouting back at the laughing, mocking crowd around him.

Emma couldn't understand a word he said. "What language is he speaking?" she asked, hardly aware that she had said it out loud.

To her surprise, Mrs. Jones answered. "French. He's from Quebec, a sailor on one o' the boats. So are some o' the people teasing him. He's lucky it's only friendly teasing. Sometimes . . ."

Her next words were drowned by a sudden uproar from the crowd.

"What did he do wrong? What's he being punished for?"

"I can't make it out. Some sort of mischief, I guess. Pillory ain't very serious punishment. Not like flogging."

As they walked away, Emma wondered whether it would be impolite to ask how Mrs. Jones came to know French. But she had no chance. The cook ordered Joe Tubb to walk in front of them so that they could pick up anything that fell out of the overloaded baskets. Then she returned to what they had been discussing before stopping near the pillory.

"We buys other food at the door during the week," Mrs. Jones told Emma as they walked. "Well, I guess you noticed that. Indians come selling fish, and the woman with fresh eggs calls on Wednesdays. And o'course the wine man and the brewer and the miller deliver. But the market gives the biggest choice and you come to know whose stuff you like – who ages his beef right and who sells fair weights and measures of things."

"Where did you learn to cook, Mrs. Jones? At home from your mother?"

"That's how I started. That was in England, o'course, near Bristol. When I was old enough to go into service I got a place in the kitchen of a big house. I was assistant cook when one of the gardeners said why didn't we get married and go to America."

"Goodness!" Emma said, because something seemed to be expected.

"We lived near New York for a while but he didn't like the Yankees so we come up to Montreal. Then he didn't get along with the French folk so we moved this way, a step at a time you might say, a job here and a job there. When he died – we were living in Kingston then – I come here and got taken on by Mrs. McPhail – better'n having to follow where a man wants to go."

"Have . . . did you ever have any children?"

"Four. They all died when they was babies."

"Oh, dear. I'm sorry."

"That's nice of you, lass, but I don't grieve over them now. It's the sort of thing that does happen."

Silently Emma agreed, thinking of the fire that had orphaned her and John.

That evening Emma was given still another kind of work to do. Mrs. McPhail had been invited out to dinner and asked Emma to sit behind the counter in the lobby of the hotel.

"Just to show a presence, you understand. Usually I sit in my own room with the door ajar so that it's obvious that there's someone on duty."

Clearly Emma herself was not to have the dignity of sitting behind the half-open door.

"You will wear one of your small aprons and keep occupied with sewing. Joseph will be in the kitchen the whole evening. If there's any trouble that needs a man's assistance, just ring for him." She indicated a small handbell standing on the counter. "And Mrs. Jones is there too."

On this chilly evening, therefore, Emma sat on a straight chair behind the counter, hemming a set of new linen table napkins. She had tidied her hair and put on a clean apron, and was pleased with the responsibility.

But she was also bored and tired. It was by now past her usual bedtime – she had seen John off to bed half an hour earlier – and besides the very plain sewing there was nothing to occupy her mind except the ponderous ticking of the clock and the quiet voices of some of the guests in the parlor.

She was also cold. The doors to the kitchen, the guests' parlor, and Mrs. McPhail's room were shut; fires burned behind all of them but none did Emma any good. She wondered how soon she might be able to afford a shawl – a good thick one, she thought, as a draft chilled her back. She blew on her fingers to warm them before once again threading the needle.

Just then the door to the parlor opened and Mrs. Heatherington came out. Emma laid aside her sewing and stood up.

"Ah, Emma. Major Heatherington and Caroline and I would like some tea, please."

"Certainly, Mrs. Heatherington. I'll bring it."

Mrs. Heatherington shivered. "Aren't you cold here?"

"A little."

"We'll leave this door open – that will help a bit."

She returned to the parlor and Emma went to the kitchen. Mrs. Jones made tea with the almost perpetually boiling water in the kettle while Emma put cups and saucers, milk, sugar, and cookies on a tray.

Only the Heatheringtons were in the parlor; grouped around the fire, they made an attractive family picture. In a rocking chair sat Caroline, tipping back and forth in short swings; she had caught a cold and had her crimson shawl wrapped around her. The vivid fabric and her blond hair were bright against the dark fabric of the fire screen behind her. Major Heatherington, on the sofa across from her, was a darker figure, but his thin face was also lit by the fire's ruddy glow. Mrs. Heatherington sat between them with a small table beside her; at Emma's approach she began to clear it so as to provide room for the tea. As Emma set down the tray, her hand brushed against Mrs. Heatherington's.

"Goodness, Emma, your hand is icy. You should be wearing a shawl."

"I suppose so," said Emma, unwilling to admit that she did not own one.

"Would you like to stay here for a minute or two to warm yourself?" Mrs. Heatherington asked as she poured the tea.

"I don't want to interrupt your conversation." She glanced around, embarrassed at the silence that her coming had caused. In any case, she ought to return to her post in the lobby.

"Not at all, not at all," said Major Heatherington, beckoning her up to the fire and then reaching to take the cup of tea that his wife was holding out to him. "We were just discussing our plans."

"Father! Surely! . . ." Caroline made an abrupt movement, which set her chair jolting even more quickly over the slightly uneven floorboards.

"Yes, I understand, Caroline. But there is nothing especially secret about them – or even very interesting, I daresay," he added, looking at Emma with the expression that was almost a smile.

Emma, more uncomfortable than ever, did not know what to answer. "I'm just new in York, sir, and I'm very interested in everything." Then she blushed at having made such a childish remark – and to the Heatheringtons, of all people, whom she admired and would like to impress!

But Mrs. Heatherington was stirring her tea and smiling at Emma. "We are also newcomers. We arrived only three weeks ago and have been too busy in York to see anything else of the country."

"Have you come to stay?" Emma asked hesitantly. Mrs. McPhail's prohibition against speaking to guests hung over her head, but if the guests began a conversation, could she be blamed?

"Oh, yes, to settle," the Major said. "We wish to purchase a farm that is already partly cleared and has a house on it, or even just a cottage. As a retired military officer, I am entitled to a tract of uncleared land but at our age, and in our station of life, we can not picture ourselves undertaking the work of clearing the forest and making a farm from the very beginning."

He paused to sip his tea. Emma, kneeling on the hearth, saw his face clearly. He was frowning, as though he were somehow dissatisfied with this plan, though it sounded sensible to Emma. She recalled her guess – her hope – that the Heatheringtons might buy the farm where she had lived, but the Major's words suggested that they would require something better.

"My husband and I love the outdoors," Mrs. Heatherington said. "Gardening, walking, flowers, wildlife. . . . We always wanted to have a country place of our own." Her lively brown face did indeed suggest outdoor activity, but Emma could not imagine her gathering potatoes or making soap.

The Major took up the story again. "Our means permit us to buy an already cleared farm and hire one or two servants, but all the same we must be as economical as possible." He spoke as if to himself and Emma thought that perhaps this need for economy explained his earlier frown.

"Yes, I see," Emma murmured. She did not express her skepticism about their finding a cottage in Upper Canada – at least a cottage such as she herself imagined them, thatched and surrounded by flowers.

Caroline sneezed violently and huddled deeper into the large crimson shawl. They all looked at her.

"Drink your tea while it's hot, Caroline," Mrs. Heatherington said, and then she looked at Emma. "Perhaps we could put a drop of whiskey in it?"

Emma was about to explain that the whiskey was locked up and that Mrs. McPhail had not left her keys behind, when Caroline protested that she hated whiskey.

"I think you should be in bed, child," the Major said. "You can take your tea with you, and maybe Emma should bring you a warming pan."

"No need, Charles," said his wife. "There's a nice fire in our room. Caroline can use our bed until we go up."

Emma's heart had sunk at the mention of fetching a warming pan because, after such an interruption, she would certainly not be included in the group again. As it turned out, Caroline was the only one to leave. She trailed away carrying her refilled teacup, and could be heard sneezing on the stairs.

"Well now," the Major resumed. "We've heard of such a

farm. Blackwood, the livery-stable man, owns it and is prepared to sell."

This was it! Emma looked from one face to the other,
waiting eagerly for more.

"A most helpful and informative man," Mrs.
Heatherington remarked, "although at first we had to
become accustomed to his bluff Yankee ways."

"Yes, we quite like Mr. Blackwood," the Major continued,
"though I don't suppose he'd ever become a personal friend.
The farm in question is two hundred acres in extent and has a
dwelling on it. Blackwood said it could be described as a
cottage and was well built and easy to heat. There is also a
sturdy barn. A substantial portion of the acreage is cleared,
though part of that area is still covered with stumps. All this
sounds very promising to us."

"And it is surrounded by woods," Mrs. Heatherington
added. "He did not mention wildflowers and animals but I'm
sure they must abound there. Except for its remoteness from
York, it seems to be what we are looking for." She smiled at
her husband.

But Emma was tense and trembling with agitation. She had
been hovering by the fire, unwilling to sit down unless invited
to. Now, afraid that her trembling might show, she crouched
again and poked the fire unnecessarily and desperately.

If this was indeed their farm, then Blackwood was lying
about it, lying scandalously! Only a few acres were cleared –
barely ten acres suitable for crops and another two with the
stumps still in the ground. The "cottage" was a tiny one-
room one-window shanty, the Andersons' first dwelling and,
though well-built as shanties went, not much more than
minimal shelter. And how could anyone possibly walk for

pleasure in the dark, silent bush where almost the only wildlife was mosquitoes and an occasional snake?

To avoid their eyes, she stared into the fire and asked, as casually as she could, "Where is this farm located, sir?"

"Some forty miles from here, almost due west. There are some close neighbors and, a mile or two distant, a small but rapidly growing village."

The Wilburs and Bateses were close, thought Emma, but Waterdown was a dreary five miles away through bush and swamp over what could not be called a road.

Mrs. Heatherington spoke. "We do feel that the distance from here is greater than we would wish. But naturally land costs less at such a remove from York."

"Naturally," Emma echoed faintly. "You have not seen this farm for yourself?"

"No – again the distance is an obstacle and the roads are so very bad. But we know of people buying land here while they themselves were still in England and being very satisfied. We feel that we can trust Mr. Blackwood. He has seen the farm and described it very clearly."

How could anyone trust Blackwood? Emma herself never had, although this was the first evidence she had found of actual dishonesty. She looked again at the Heatheringtons; the Major was eating a cookie and Mrs. Heatherington drinking tea. They were kind and warm-hearted people and Emma couldn't bear to think that they should be hurt.

She had drawn her breath to tell them the facts that would protect them when she recalled seeing, two weeks ago, Mr. Blackwood walking up the driveway of the Wilburs' farm with Mrs. McPhail's hand tucked in his arm and their two heads leaning together in close and quiet talk. She had sensed conspiracy then, and suddenly she knew that revealing Blackwood's dishonesty meant revealing her own connection with the farm and also involving Mrs. McPhail – who was after all her guardian, employer, and aunt. Though she could not imagine the consequences very precisely, she could almost hear them reverberating like angry thunder around her. She must think further before speaking, though her anguished desire to protect the Heatheringtons made her hands clench into fists.

"Have you discussed these plans with your friends here – with people who might know the area or . . . or have had dealings with Mr. Blackwood?"

"Oh, they've all had dealings with Blackwood – rented horses from him, you know. He's well known."

"Our friends," said Mrs. Heatherington, "all approve of the plan and have promised to come and visit us next summer. If the cottage is too small to accommodate guests they will bring tents. Being military men, most of them, they are used to living in primitive conditions. One will bring his flute and we will have concerts in the wilderness."

Emma was silent, searching for words. Then she began hesitantly, "Of course you may find . . ."

"Now Emma thinks we're complete fools," the Major said with a smile. "We know that it will not be all visits and concerts. We are prepared for hardships. Living in garrisons has taught us a great deal."

If they thought that the farm as Blackwood described it would mean living in hardship, how would they regard it as it actually was? Emma could imagine their disillusionment and longed to help them, but she dared not say a word until she had considered the consequences more carefully.

"And your daughter?" she asked, mainly to keep the conversation going. The Heatheringtons did not know that she had overheard their talk last week.

Mrs. Heatherington answered. "You are thinking, perhaps, that she is not the material of which pioneers are made. Of course she was not with us on our more difficult postings. She lived with relatives in England. But she will – we're almost certain – marry an officer serving at the fort and will stay here in York."

"You must be very happy about that."

As Emma spoke, the front door crashed open, reminding her that she was supposed to be on duty in the lobby. Quickly she excused herself, more than glad to escape for a moment her dilemma about whether to tell the Heatheringtons the truth about the farm. She longed to be free to help them, to talk to them about her parents' experience on the farm and about Blackwood's deception, but she was afraid that she might never be able to tell all of it.

In the lobby was Mr. Tufts, struggling to undo the collar of his cape. Emma realized at once that he was very drunk; she smelled it and she saw it in his struggle with the fastening. She dodged behind the counter.

"Come on, gi's a hand here," he mumbled, apparently to her.

Emma hesitated, wondering whether her duties in the hotel included such a task as this. She thought of ringing the bell for Joseph Tubb. But just then Tufts shouted, "Come on, come on!" and began pulling at his cloak. Something ripped but the collar did not come undone.

In the parlor doorway, Major Heatherington appeared. He gave one glance at Emma and then advanced on Tufts. "Here, man, I'll help you," he said in a manner quite different from the rather thoughtful, almost indecisive one that Emma had seen earlier. She realized that for all his appearance of naïveté and idealism, all his trust in Blackwood, he was also a man of action, used to dealing with other men. He could size up Tufts' condition quickly and deal with it. Now he unbuttoned the man's collar, pulled the cape off him, and hung it on a peg. Then he helped him up the stairs. Mrs. Heatherington followed, wishing Emma good night as she passed.

Half an hour later, when Mrs. McPhail had come home and the evening's duty was over, Emma went upstairs too and stood beside the pallet in the attic where John slept. It had occurred to her that John might be in danger from Blackwood's business practices. She would have liked to warn him at this very minute, before any more time passed, to be on his guard. But he was fast asleep, curled like a puppy under the covers, his sandy hair tumbled, and before her candle or her mere presence could wake him she went on to her own room.

The quarter-pie window was black, reflecting only herself, white-faced and dark-eyed in the single candle flame. A window on the outside world, a mirror for herself – how strange and solemn it was to have a window all her own, a view that was shared by no one else.

The cold soon interrupted such thoughts and drove her into bed.

When she was under the covers and slowly warming up, she reviewed the evening's events and the problem about her own loyalties. She was tense, and her mind wouldn't rest although she knew that it was very late.

It had been a difficult evening. No longer could she look forward with unmixed pleasure to the Heatheringtons living on the farm – Blackwood's dishonesty had spoiled that. Indeed, if Emma revealed the facts, the Heatheringtons would probably stop dealing with him and look for another farm.

But all the same she had been sorry when the evening ended. She had liked being with the Heatheringtons – it had been a sort of family gathering. Life in the hotel would not offer her many occasions of this kind. And the Heatheringtons had, for some reason, not treated her like a servant. Emma had always heard that English gentlefolk were very class conscious but except for the fetching of tea she had not been aware of being a chambermaid. True, she had not felt free to sit down unless invited to, but she might have been too scrupulous in that.

All these were details. The essential thing was the Heatheringtons' manner. They had drawn her in, told her about themselves, treated her simply as a new friend. As she remembered the feeling, Emma forgot her perplexities about the farm in a flood of gratitude. They could only have treated her like that, she thought, if they had recognized something worthwhile in her and disregarded the apron and what it represented.

Somehow she would have to help them. She had information that they needed, the true information about the farm. And, if possible, she would give them a hint about Blackwood. She would have to do it soon.

Then abruptly she stiffened and opened her eyes to stare into the darkness. Mr. Blackwood would sell the farm at a profit and, if Emma's conjectures were right, would share that profit with Mrs. McPhail.

She remembered how suspicious she had been in the beginning of Mrs. McPhail's refusal to talk about herself, her life in York, and her plans for Emma and John. She remembered Mr. Blackwood coming to inspect the farm, certainly by an earlier arrangement between him and Mrs. McPhail, and her strong sense that there was a connivance or conspiracy between them and that Mrs. McPhail was the cleverer one, the leader.

And now Emma knew why Mrs. McPhail, as one of Martin Anderson's heirs and his children's guardian, had been so keen to sell the farm to Blackwood, and why the selling price, though fair, was rather low, and why Blackwood had given the Heatheringtons such a glorified picture of the farm.

Mrs. McPhail had received one-quarter of the price that Blackwood had paid for the farm. That was what Martin Anderson had determined in his will. But when the farm was resold, Mr. Blackwood would make a quick and, probably, large profit. Mrs. McPhail would share that profit and therefore would get a greater portion of the farm's value than her half-brother's will had bequeathed to her.

No wonder she had looked so smug about everything to do with the farm. And, with Emma working hard for her, and even John doing a few chores in the hotel before and after his daily stint at the livery stable, no wonder she was pleased to be their guardian. Mrs. McPhail, instead of being burdened, was benefiting at every turn.

Emma, wide awake and indignant, could not help admiring her aunt a little. But she was glad to have spotted what was going on. She did not know yet how she could use this information but she would find a way.

SEVEN

Books

On the following morning Emma woke with the feeling that she had to act quickly so as to avert some disaster. In a moment she remembered: she had to find a way to tell the Heatheringtons the truth about the farm but she must do it in such a way that Mrs. McPhail would never find out. Of course the Heatheringtons wouldn't deliberately betray her, but as soon as they revealed their new knowledge about the farm Blackwood would suspect something. And then undoubtedly Emma, and maybe John as well, would be punished.

Sleeping on the problem had brought no solution.

But during breakfast she learned something that eased the pressure. One of the guests asked Mrs. McPhail a question and in reply was told that Mr. Blackwood was away on business for a few days.

Emma took a deep breath of relief. No deal about the farm could be made until he returned; she herself had a spell of time in which she could quietly work out what was best to do. She wished there were someone to discuss it with but could think of no one.

On Monday afternoon she was temporarily distracted from these worries. While she was helping Mrs. Tubb take the laundry off the line, there was a commotion at the gate. She turned in time to see John being dragged in by a furious man with spectacles pushed up into his hair and an inky streak down the side of his face. John was looking sullen and had a cut on his temple. Behind them was a handful of boys, shouting and scuffling among themselves.

Emma ran forward.

"What are you doing with my brother?" she demanded.

"Oh, he's your brother, is he? Well, keep him away from cockfights, then."

"Cockfights!" she exclaimed, staring from him to John and back again. "And who are you, sir?"

"Crab. I run Crab's School." He gestured vaguely with his free hand. "I've told the boys over and over that I won't have them staging cockfights behind the school. And just when I'm making some headway, your brother and his like start them at it again. Don't you have a father? I should be talking to him."

"No, sir, we don't."

This silenced the angry schoolmaster for a moment. Emma pulled John from his grasp and held him against her. She saw that he was frightened as well as sullen, and she was anxious to do something about the cut on his face.

The man mopped his face with his sleeve, thus adding dirt to the ink and perspiration. He looked at Emma as though trying to assess her age and responsibility; clearly the fading of his anger weakened his will to take the matter further.

"Look you, miss, make sure that your brother stays out of my schoolyard. He's not a pupil of mine and has no business there. And tell him to keep away from cockfighting and . . . ," he apparently became aware for the first time of the boys who had been following him, "and away from this sort of rabble."

"Yes, sir," Emma said without submissiveness. "Good day to you."

She took John upstairs and bathed the cut. It was not serious, she was glad to see, but he was trembling and glad to sit down on her bed. She fetched him bread and jam from the kitchen and made him sit quietly beside her to eat it.

"Tell me what happened," she invited.

"I didn't do what that man said, start the other boys cock-fighting."

"I was sure you didn't."

"They already had the birds fighting, behind the shed in the schoolyard. I was walking along the street after doing an errand for Fred – Mr. Blackwood's away."

"Yes, I'd heard."

"Well, I heard something going on, and went to see. I guess the boys bring the birds in covered baskets and hide them behind the shed until school's over. There were lots of boys there, all crowded around and shouting and . . . sort of betting, you know, without money."

"I know."

"And then the man, the schoolmaster, came out and some of the boys rushed to gather everything up, the birds and baskets and everything. The rest of us ran. I tripped and fell. That's how I got hurt. He picked me up. I told him I lived here. I was sure hoping that Mrs. McPhail wouldn't be around." At that he grinned. The food was doing him good.

"Did you like the cockfighting?"

His face darkened. "It's pretty vicious. I guess they sharpen the birds' spurs or something. They – the birds, I mean – jump and slash each other. Both of them were bleeding and had lost some feathers by the time it was stopped." John shuddered and pressed closer against Emma. "It's horrid to make creatures do that to each other."

"Cocks fight in barnyards, though," she said, testing him a bit.

"But Father told me that that's nature's way of making sure that it's the best cock who guards the hens. And the loser can run away. One of these that I saw behind the school wanted to run but the boys pushed him back in to keep fighting."

"Well, I guess you won't go out of your way to watch a cockfight again."

"No." He got up off the bed. "I'd better go back to work. Fred'll be looking for me."

"Are you feeling all right now? Does that cut hurt?"

"Not much. Be seeing you."

Cockfighting! Emma exclaimed to herself as she went downstairs. But she was actually pleased that John had seen it and been revolted by it. That very revulsion was another bit of a safeguard for him, something to help form his character and steer him through the complications of being young and strange in a town as big as York.

The following afternoon Mrs. McPhail asked Emma to deliver an order to the wine merchant. Emma did so and then, on her way home, stopped outside Mr. Lesslie's store to look at the display of books. Again there was a book lying open; Emma had read half a page of a biography of John Milton when she was joined by Miss Morgan.

"Hello there, Emma."

"Oh, hello, Miss Morgan."

"Gloating over the books, I see. I do that too."

"But you *have* books."

"There are always others that I'd like to own. I'm on my way back to the hotel. Are you?"

"Yes."

"Come along, then. We'll go together."

Emma remembered her fears, on that first day in the hotel, that as a chambermaid she would have no contact with the guests. She was pleased to discover again how wrong she had been, even as she recalled Mrs. McPhail's warning against talking to the guests. But Mrs. McPhail had prohibited *personal* conversation – and in any case, Emma had an idea that her recent talk with the Heatheringtons had already broken all the rules. So far she had, however, obeyed Mrs. McPhail's unstated desire to conceal the fact that they were aunt and niece.

So it was with a mixture of apprehension and pleasure that she accompanied Miss Morgan.

"I gather that you can read?" Miss Morgan asked.

"Oh, yes, my father taught me."

"Good for him," Miss Morgan said decidedly. "I think education for girls is very important. They are, after all, the mothers of the next generation." She glanced at Emma. "That's what I'm here for, you know. To try to start a girls' school. I'm from New Hampshire – my father was a clergyman but both my parents are dead now – and I'm staying in the hotel while looking for a suitable building and talking to people to find out what the prospects of success might be. Asking about potential pupils, you know."

"Do you think there will be enough pupils?"

"I think so. Of course there's already one school for girls, run by a Miss Purcell, and some girls attend the Common School, but the College – which is for boys only – is more or less replacing a school that was attended by girls as well as boys. Clearly there is room for another girls' school. My main concern now is to find a house."

"I hope you succeed, Miss Morgan. I would have liked to go to school when I was young."

Miss Morgan laughed. "You talk as though you were no longer young."

"Oh, I'm not. I have my brother and myself to look after and as you saw the other day, men consider me grown up."

"Oh, men! Don't pay too much attention to them. But are you and your brother completely alone in the world? No relatives at all? What happened to your parents?"

This was very blunt but Emma felt that it was motivated by good nature and genuine interest.

"They died last winter in a fire." Afraid of being asked again about other relatives, she steered the conversation in another direction. "Do you know of any place, here in York, where I could borrow books?"

"I don't believe there is, but there's talk of starting a Mechanics' Institute."

"Mechanics?" Emma asked, thinking of laboring men and lessons in carpentry. How could such a place be of any use to her?

"It will be an organization offering lectures and a reading room – a sort of informal education for working people."

"Women too?"

"Yes, indeed."

"But it's not been started yet?"

"No, the founding meeting is to be held next month. In the meantime, would you like to borrow one of my books?"

"Oh, yes, please!" Every time she cleaned Miss Morgan's room, Emma spent a moment looking at the books. She had opened one or two but, knowing that it was wrong, had found no pleasure in it.

Now, however, she remembered something else to spoil the prospect. "But I don't have much time for reading. It might take me a long while to finish it."

"Don't worry about that. Most novels come in several small volumes, as you probably know. You can borrow the volumes one by one. How much time do you have to yourself?"

"Sometimes an hour or two in the afternoon. In the evenings I usually go to bed as soon as I've finished work."

"I can well believe it. Mrs. McPhail would make you work. She's an impressive woman, though, don't you think?"

"Yes, she is," Emma said politely.

Miss Morgan gave her a keen look. "That's right, better not to talk about your employer." She went up the steps of the hotel's veranda. "Can you come upstairs now to choose a book?"

Emma was still standing on the street. "Yes, but . . . if you don't mind, I'll go in by the kitchen door and then up to your room." She flushed as she said it, angry that the social division should appear again.

"Of course, whatever you like."

Something cool in Miss Morgan's last words made Emma wonder whether after all the lady's friendliness had been merely a passing thing, but when she reached the bedroom everything was comfortable again. They talked for a few minutes about the books on the shelf and others that they had read. "These are mainly novels and poetry," said Miss Morgan, tapping her finger along the embossed leather spines. "I have more books packed and stored at home, ready to be sent here when I settle."

"My father liked essays, Addison and Steele and Samuel Johnson. But I enjoy novels too. Have you read *Tom Jones*?"

"Yes, though my mother was not sure that it was suitable for girls."

"Neither was mine, but she didn't object very hard."

Their eyes met in shared amusement.

"What about *Pamela*?" Miss Morgan asked, picking up and opening a small book. "Would you like to borrow this? It's about a servant girl whose employer makes attempts on her virtue. I won't tell you how it ends but I can assure you that there's nothing your parents would have objected to – not if they allowed *Tom Jones*. But you may not want to read about servants in a big house in England?"

"Oh, yes, I'd like to," said Emma, taking the book.

"Remember that it is only a novel, an imaginary story. You'll find that there are some things in it that don't sound very believable but they're probably put there to make the story work. If you like, we can talk about it when you've finished the first volume."

"That would be wonderful."

Miss Morgan put a brown paper cover around the outside of the book and Emma took it up to her room before returning downstairs to report to Mrs. McPhail that the wine would be delivered before dinner tomorrow.

In the kitchen she found Mrs. Delaney having a cup of tea with Mrs. Jones. Mrs. Delaney said she was just leaving; she finished her tea and then drew Emma out into the yard with her. At the gate they stopped.

"Any sign yet of your aunt having a position for me?" Mrs. Delaney asked, laying her hand on Emma's arm.

"I don't think so," Emma said, somewhat puzzled. "You should ask her yourself. She's in her room now – I spoke to her a few minutes ago."

"But you, as her niece . . ."

Emma suppressed her annoyance and growing uneasiness. Something was going on here that she didn't understand.

"You are an old friend, though, Mrs. Delaney. That will have much more weight with her. She doesn't seem eager to acknowledge that I am related to her."

Mrs. Delaney darted a look at Emma and then frowned in thought. Emma was reminded of a squirrel snatching a piece of food and holding it firmly and secretively for later use.

"I got another reason for coming to see you," said Mrs. Delaney after a moment. "Something I heard that'd interest you. I *had* thought we could exchange favors . . . but never mind."

Emma was becoming even more uncomfortable. She had
no idea what Mrs. Delaney was up to and had no wish to have
her back in the hotel. Every impulse urged her to shake
herself free of this woman, and perhaps some expression in
her face or some movement in her arm conveyed that to Mrs.
Delaney. Whatever it was, the woman leaned closer and said,
"It's information about your Mother'n Father."

Emma's heart leapt but she knew she had to handle this
cautiously. How she wished she could say that she knew all
about her parents! – but the few words she had exchanged
with Mrs. McPhail on the subject, and the door that had then
been shut in her face, had made her realize how little she
knew and how dearly she wanted to learn more. Being ignorant put her in a weak position, just as having information
would have made her strong.

"Oh, yes?" she said, trying to sound casual.

"I don't know whether to tell you what I learned," said
Mrs. Delaney rather sulkily.

"You must decide that for yourself," said Emma as coolly as
possible, though her mind itched to know what the information could be. "But keeping it to yourself won't increase my
influence with Mrs. McPhail. The two things are completely
separate. So we don't seem to be able to go any further."

They both watched Mrs. Jones cross the yard to speak to
Joseph Tubb, who was picking late apples from one of the trees.
When the cook had returned to the kitchen, Mrs. Delaney
turned to Emma again, tightening the grip on her arm.

"Jack O'Brien, at the Anchor, knows something about your
folks. Go talk to him." And after a final squeeze she released
Emma and walked away down the street.

Emma remained where she was, transfixed with surprise. Whatever she had expected, it wasn't this.

If only she had known earlier, she could have gone to the Anchor today. Now she would have to wait until her next free afternoon. She was annoyed and deeply puzzled when she went indoors to help prepare for dinner.

EIGHT

Mrs. Delaney

The talk with Mrs. Delaney had occurred on Tuesday. On Wednesday Emma was unable to go to the Anchor because Mrs. Jones set her to work peeling, coring, and stringing apples to be dried. When the thin segments were strung like beads on a thread, Mrs. Jones dipped them in hot water to preserve the color and then hung them between the ceiling beams to dry.

While working, Emma had time to think – or rather, to worry. A remark of John's that morning had revealed that Mr. Blackwood was expected to return on Saturday; soon after that the Heatheringtons would presumably continue their negotiations for buying the farm. She *had* to talk to them before that – and yet she had not worked out a way to tell them what they needed to know without disclosing more than she ought to about herself and Mrs. McPhail. There was a further problem, too: if she spoke now, she left herself open to the question of why she had delayed so long.

It was not only Blackwood, apparently, who was pulling the wool over the Heatheringtons' eyes. Caroline was still – or again – doing things of which her parents would surely disapprove. The evening before, in the attic, while Emma was mending a tear in John's shirt, John had mentioned that Miss Heatherington had several times gone out with Captain Marshall in a carriage hired from Blackwood's stable.

"You're sure it was Marshall? Not Captain Dixon?"

"Oh, no, it's Marshall all right. Mr. Blackwood calls him that. When I hand him the reins he winks at me and sometimes gives me a tip."

"What are you doing with the tips?" Emma asked with a twinge of jealousy. She herself received no tips.

"Special hiding place," he said, jerking his head toward the end of the attic where he slept.

"Just don't put them in one of those pieces of furniture. You never know when they might be used again or sold."

"No, they're in a hole in a rafter."

"Good. But listen, does Miss Heatherington come to the stable with Captain Marshall?"

"No."

"Well, then, how do you know they go together?"

"I've seen them in town. They aren't really hiding it."

Because he spent part of each day running errands, John knew far more about York than Emma did. He had been to the fort and the wharves and most of the important houses, and in these three weeks had quite overcome his initial fears.

"What are you going to do with the money . . . the tips?"

she asked a few minutes later, when she had shaken out the shirt and held it up to look for more holes or tears.

"Save it," he said without hesitation. "I don't ever want to be without money again. I always have a penny or two in my pocket now, just in case, but I hardly ever spend that. I just like knowing it's there." As an afterthought, he said, "You can borrow some if you need it."

"Thanks, John. I might have to do that sometime." Then she had told him that she was on the track of information about their parents but had not yet been able to go and talk to the landlord of the Anchor.

"O'Brien?" said John sharply, looking up at her. "You watch out for him."

"Why?"

"Oh, well, I've heard things. Don't go to that tavern of his in the evening. It's no place for a girl."

He was right, of course. Emma remembered how uneasy she had been when she was there with Mrs. Delaney – and that was in the afternoon. Obviously John knew what he was talking about. This was the steady, sensible John she had known before the upheaval of the past summer, who had always given the impression of being older than his years and who now was augmenting his native good sense with experience of town life.

"What do you think of Mr. Blackwood?" she asked.

"I don't like him but he certainly is a smooth one. You should see him with the customers – jolly with the jolly ones, talking about hunting or racing with the sporting types, gallant to the ladies . . ." John shook his head in awed admiration.

Now, at the kitchen table, as she took another apple from the large basket and cut it into quarters before peeling, coring, and slicing it, Emma wondered if it was behavior like this that had taken in the Heatheringtons. She herself saw through Blackwood, but then he had never flattered her – and, even if he had, she thought that her instinct would have warned her. The Heatheringtons seemed to accept him as just another of the curious specimens native to a world that was altogether new and strange to them.

That day and the following one she hardly saw the Heatheringtons. John reported that they had attended a horse race organized by the officers of the garrison. Emma herself overheard them discussing what they would wear to a dinner and dance at Government House. Emma encountered them only at breakfast and had no chance to speak to them privately, so that even if she had known how to warn them she would have had no opportunity.

On Thursday evening, during dinner, Emma heard Miss Morgan tell Mrs. McPhail about finding a house in which to locate her school.

"You must be pleased," commented Mrs. McPhail as she carefully carved a roast of beef and arranged the slices on a platter.

"It's not as simple as that," said Miss Morgan with an angry little laugh. "I'm not able to take it after all."

Emma, standing beside Mrs. McPhail and waiting to hand the platter of beef around, longed to hear more. Fortunately Mrs. McPhail, rather absentmindedly, said the right things to elicit the whole story.

"I considered it almost a miracle to have found such a roomy house empty," said Miss Morgan. "A handsome building – rather low but with large rooms on the ground floor and six bedrooms upstairs. I was about to sign the lease when my lawyer asked where the house was located."

Miss Morgan paused for effect and then went on. "I said that it was on Berkeley Street, in the eastern part of town. He advised me against taking it. The air, it seems, is unhealthful so close to the marshes at the mouth of the Don River – there is a good deal of ague and malaria in the region. It certainly is no place for a school. I wish I had known about that before."

She glanced around as though looking for sympathy – or perhaps for someone to blame – but besides Mrs. McPhail and Emma the only people in the room were three middle-aged men who were apparently deep in their own thoughts.

However Mrs. McPhail, who had finished the carving, was looking at Miss Morgan with a speculative expression. "Did the lawyer definitely advise you not to take it?"

"He suggested that I reconsider. It seems that there is no way in which an owner can be compelled to tell a prospective tenant or buyer about such drawbacks." She laughed again but not in amusement. "'Buyer beware,' he said."

"I believe that is true."

Miss Morgan reflected a moment and then spoke less angrily. "It was a very attractive house. It's a pity that such buildings should stand empty. Someone built it – put a lot of planning and money and work into it and even love maybe – and now it's at the mercy of mice and wind and rot."

"Perhaps you should reconsider once again and think about taking it," Mrs. McPhail suggested. "After all, there are people living in the area. Most of the houses are inhabited, I believe."

"I could not risk it with a school," said Miss Morgan firmly.

Those words about the sadness of abandoned houses stayed in Emma's mind. The farm where she had grown up was also lying empty now, and she still had not talked to the Heatheringtons.

Early the following morning, when Emma was sweeping the lobby, Mrs. Delaney walked in. Emma was struck by her almost aggressive air; she wore a new-looking hat and strode confidently to the counter, behind which she quickly established herself. Clearly she was once more on the hotel staff.

The details came later that morning from Mrs. Jones, who had managed to get information from Mrs. McPhail while discussing the day's menu.

"Mrs. Delaney is lodging just along the street and'll come in three or four days a week, doing some of Mrs. McPhail's work. Nothing dirty, just ladylike things."

So she managed it after all, Emma thought resentfully. "You don't like her much, do you?" she asked Mrs. Jones.

"She didn't make herself popular when she looked after the place for Mrs. McPhail. Old Harriet ain't always pleasant but she's fair and knows her job. Delaney *acts* friendly when she wants to but you never know where you are with 'er."

"Old Harriet?" Emma asked.

Mrs. Jones gave a wry smile. "Well, the devil's called old Harry, ain't he? We call her Old Harriet when she gets across us. Like now."

"Has she got across us? You mean by hiring Mrs. Delaney?"

"Not just that. There's more. It ain't happened yet but I smell something in the wind. It seems Old Harriet needs an assistant 'cause she's been asked to join a committee to look after immigrants. D'you know about that? I guess it's sort of an honor, though it looks like bringing more work than thanks. To us as well as her."

"What sort of immigrants? Why do they need looking after?"

"Oh, you see 'em down at the wharves sometimes, just standing there and staring. They got no job to go to, haven't taken up or bought any land to settle on, just trust to the good Lord. Mind you, that's only *some* immigrants." Mrs. Jones laughed. "Nice for Mrs. McPhail to be the good Lord to 'em!"

"And with winter coming on, too," Emma said, mainly to herself, thinking of the immigrants and remembering how helpless and destitute she had been after the fire, on that cold day in early March.

That conversation with Mrs. Jones took place on Friday, the day on which Emma cleaned Mrs. McPhail's rooms. Mrs. McPhail was not there when Emma went to perform that task, but Mrs. Delaney was, writing at the desk. Emma – who had been about to push open the door, which was standing ajar by an inch or two – paused for a moment and watched Mrs. Delaney dip her pen in the ink.

This was how Emma had pictured herself being employed in the hotel. Now here she was, standing with the broom and dustpan in one hand and the basket of dust cloths in the other, to do the cleaning – and there was Mrs. Delaney at the writing desk. For the first time in that busy morning, Emma realized that Mrs. Delaney's return to the hotel staff would restrict her own chance for improving her position. She would be confined to the menial work that, according to Mrs. Jones, Mrs. Delaney would not be doing.

On this occasion at least, Mrs. Delaney was not wearing an apron.

Emma wondered whether she was expected to go away and come back later, after Mrs. Delaney had finished whatever she was doing. But something stubborn in her refused to change her routine unless told to. She put down the basket and knocked at the door.

Mrs. Delaney looked up.

"I usually do Mrs. McPhail's rooms now."

"Oh! Yes, o'course, it's Friday, ain't it?" said Mrs. Delaney with the air of one who is above such things as household routines. "I can take my work to the counter out there." She gave a little laugh. "Account books're easy to move."

She carried the ledger to the counter in the lobby. Emma had a moment of rather shame-faced satisfaction in seeing that Mrs. Delaney would now have to stand rather than sit at her work.

When Emma had cleaned the two rooms, she paused alongside the counter where Mrs. Delaney was still busy.

"I'm finished in there, Mrs. Delaney."

"Thank you, Emma."

Emma lingered a moment longer. "I haven't had a free moment since Tuesday to go to the Anchor. Did Mr. O'Brien actually tell you anything about my parents or just say that he had the information? And how did he know that I was their daughter?"

"He overheard us that day when you and me were having a drink. I forget what we said but I guess we talked about Mrs. McPhail. He knows her, o'course – not well but the way you do know people in a town like this."

"But what does he know about . . . ?"

"Sorry, Emma, you'll have to ask him for yourself." And with a smile in which there was no friendliness, she began moving her work back to the desk.

Emma went through the rest of the day – which again included the whole afternoon peeling apples – depressed and tense. She realized only now how much she had counted on her position as chambermaid being temporary, on a speedy promotion to the sort of work that Mrs. Delaney was now doing.

Mr. Blackwood was expected back tomorrow, and the Heatheringtons were out so much that she despaired of finding a chance to speak with them.

When, at the end of the afternoon, she went up to her room to tidy herself before serving dinner, she leaned her forehead for a moment against the cold glass of the quarter-pie window. It wouldn't do to cry now because she had to return to the kitchen in a few minutes, but she could have wept with frustration and misery. Even the sight of Miss Morgan's book – of which she had read the first few pages last night with great pleasure – didn't cheer her up.

NINE

Revelation

When Emma woke up the next morning she had a cold. Her nose was stuffed and her throat sore. She would have to take all three of her handkerchiefs downstairs with her, and perhaps borrow one from John. As soon as they were dirty she'd have to wash them, and she'd see if Mrs. Jones had any clean rags that could be used while the hand-kerchiefs were drying.

That was the beginning of a day plagued by mishaps and extra work for all the servants. One of the guests left his room in such a filthy state that it took Emma much longer than usual to clean it. Mrs. Jones had barely returned from the market when a wagon drove up to the door selling dead pigeons, shot from the migrating flocks. Because potted pigeon was one of the hotel's specialties, Mrs. Jones bought several dozen. They had to be cleaned and prepared for potting – in addition to all the usual work.

Emma was saved from having to help with the gruesome work of cleaning the dead birds only because Mrs. McPhail told her that morning to wash the outsides of the windows, a job that of course had to be done before the winter. Being up on a ladder was only slightly less horrible than plucking and eviscerating pigeons but at least it allowed her to enjoy the weather. It was an unexpectedly warm day, sunny but hazy, and she agreed with the passer-by who shouted at her, "Indian summer, lass!"

For a while Joseph Tubb was there to help move the heavy ladder from window to window and steady it while she climbed. But then a man came to see him, a lumberyard owner who claimed that young Joe had done some damage in his yard the night before. Only Mrs. Jones' solemn word that Joe had been in bed with a feverish cold, for which she had made him a medicinal drink, persuaded the man that Joe was not the culprit. The whole argument took place in the yard so that Emma, washing the windows on that side, heard every word.

In the afternoon she continued with the apples. She would have liked to take the work outdoors but couldn't because the peeled apples attracted flies and wasps, active again because of the summery weather. The kitchen was hot with the fire needed for cooking the pigeons, but at least there were fewer flies.

After some time, Emma dropped her paring knife to catch a couple of sneezes, then arched her back to ease the aching muscles. She also flexed her hands, the skin of which was puckered by the tart juice of the apples. It was a hateful feeling. In fact, she was one mass of discomfort today.

Mrs. Jones, taking a moment's rest, sat down near her. "You got neat fingers, girl. I can't remember when I seen apples done that pretty. But I don't like the sound of that cold. I'll make you my hot drink."

"I couldn't drink anything hot in this weather," Emma said fretfully, lifting the single heavy braid of hair off her neck.

"It's good for you – helps you sweat out the sickness. And I think you should lay down on bed for a while before dinner."

Emma glanced doubtfully at her. "I'd love to, but are you sure that would be all right?"

Mrs. Jones put on a stubborn face that Emma knew well. "It better be all right. I'll see to it. You got to get over that cold, else you'll be sick in bed like Joe. Finish stringing them last bits and then you go up and rest. I'll give you the drink along." She got up and took a large cup from one of the open shelves of the cupboard.

Emma had strung the last slices and was blowing her nose again when Mrs. Tubb came in from the back kitchen, where she had been doing the laundry. She was supporting one hand with the other.

"Someone else'll have to do the rest," she said abruptly, plopping down on the bench alongside the table and rubbing her right wrist.

"What's the matter?" asked Mrs. Jones.

"Hurt my hand tipping a bucket."

"Let's see it," said Mrs. Jones. She felt and moved the hand and wrist, while Mrs. Tubb's inexpressive face twitched. "Ain't nothing broken, I'd say."

"I can't finish the wash, though."

The two women and Emma looked at each other. "I'll do it," said Emma, reluctantly renouncing the promised rest.

"You and me together," said Mrs. Jones. "Here, Mrs. Tubb, you keep the fire going. Don't build it up any higher, just keep it where it is now. And if you see the mistress, tell her about your hand."

Mrs. Jones and Emma went through the connecting door to the back kitchen. It was hot from the fire that had heated the wash water. Two tubs, one of suds and one of rinse water, were placed on a low platform. A steaming kettle stood beside the rinse tub, which was half full of cold, clean water.

"I'll finish filling that tub. You carry on washing," said Mrs. Jones.

So Emma plunged her already puckered hands into the warm soapy water, rubbed the cloth against the washboard, wrung towels and sheets, and dropped them in the other tub. Mrs. Jones rinsed them and hung them on the line in the yard.

They finished the laundry and tidied the back kitchen, then stood outdoors for a moment watching Joseph split firewood.

"It'll take that laundry a while to dry with no wind," Mrs. Jones commented as they plodded back to the kitchen.

On such a day Emma would have liked to have a good wash before dinner, but there was no time to do anything more than tidy her hair and rub Mrs. Jones' homemade salve on her hands. Then, numb with exhaustion and other miseries, she set the table, served dinner, carried a tray up to an elderly guest who preferred to eat in his own room, cleared the table, and managed to eat a bit of dinner herself. Her head was thick with the cold and her ears rang. Her nose was red and sore from being blown all day. She longed for bed, even though her room would be hot after the day-long sunshine on the roof.

When she had finished her work, she took her candle and went slowly up the stairs, first the flight from the lobby and then the one to the attic, pulling herself up by the railing. Halfway up the second flight she suddenly felt a stab of pain in the palm of her hand. It was a splinter.

This was too much. She sat down on the stairs and burst into tears, leaning her head against the wall and blowing her nose into an already damp and crumpled piece of cloth from Mrs. Jones' ragbag.

There Mrs. Heatherington found her a few minutes later, having heard the sobbing and opened the door at the bottom of the stairs to investigate. That lady came briskly up the steps and sat down beside Emma.

"What is it, my dear? Shall I call Mrs. McPhail?"

Emma shook her head, thinking bitterly that Mrs. McPhail wouldn't be much comfort at a moment like this. Mrs. Jones would be the one to ask for, but she was also exhausted after a particularly tiring day.

Mrs. Heatherington spoke again. "Oh, you've hurt your hand. A splinter. I see it very plainly. Come to our room and I'll get it out for you."

The Heatheringtons' room was cool and airy, making Emma realize anew how uncomfortable she had been all day. She sat down on the bed, as Mrs. Heatherington directed her, and blew her nose. Only then did she remember that, before going to bed, she still had to wash the handkerchiefs and rags she had used that day and hope that they would be dry by tomorrow morning.

Mrs. Heatherington had pulled up a chair and now, with needle and tweezers, she began to dig for the splinter in Emma's hand. The pain made Emma's eyes water, but by pressing her fist to her lips she managed to keep silent. Automatically trying to distract herself, she noticed that the door to Caroline's room was half open and that the candle-light touched the usual luxurious litter beyond. The Major and his daughter must be downstairs still; they sometimes played cards after dinner.

"Here it is!" Mrs. Heatherington exclaimed, showing the tweezers with a large splinter in them, while Emma dabbed at her bloody hand with the sodden cloth. "Now, where did I put the bandages?"

Mrs. Heatherington applied ointment and tied a neat bandage around the hand. "Don't get that wet for a day or two, and then let me look at it again."

"Thank you." Emma managed a smile but then had to blow her nose again. She knew she should leave now. But such kindness as this had been rare in her life recently. Having had to do without her parents' care and guidance for more than six months, having to decide things for herself – which included deciding which adults to believe and trust – had been more of a strain than she realized. Emma could not bring herself to leave just yet and, as unspoken excuse, occupied herself in blowing her nose thoroughly.

"I'm afraid the bandage will prevent you from doing certain kinds of work for a few days," Mrs. Heatherington said.

Emma pictured Mrs. McPhail's cold disapproval of any rearrangement of tasks for such a reason. "I doubt if that can be managed," she said. "I'll have to do the usual things, and finish the windows and the apples. . . ." She sneezed and then, as the hopeless misery overcame her again, sobbed into the wet cloth.

A moment later the cloth was taken from her hand and a clean, well-ironed handkerchief pushed into its place. Mrs.

Heatherington sat down on the bed and put an arm around Emma. "Does Mrs. McPhail give you too much to do?"

"The days are long and busy," Emma said awkwardly after a moment, not wanting to complain. And with that her mind began reviving, as though this sympathy had eased the numbness of exhaustion.

"Do you have any free time?"

"Sometimes an hour or two in the afternoon, if there's nothing else to be done. But usually there *is* something else – mending linen, or preparing the apples for drying, or helping Mrs. Tubb polish silver. . . ."

"Yes," said Mrs. Heatherington, "that's what happens in small establishments with only a few servants. You poor child. But surely things will improve. You are starting on the lowest rung."

"What is there to be promoted to? I don't want to be a cook like Mrs. Jones. I had hoped to do some of the desk work someday, but now Mrs. Delaney has been hired for that. It looks as though I'll be a chambermaid forever." She had an impulse to imitate John and burrow against Mrs. Heatherington for comfort but she had no right to do that. So she merely clenched hard inside herself and tried to keep down the welling tears.

"Have you no mother, my dear? Or guardian? You're very young to be entirely on your own."

"My parents are dead." She paused, realizing that this was the opening she needed but still hesitating before doing what would certainly bring Mrs. McPhail's wrath down on her. After this evening's kindness, however, she owed something to Mrs. Heatherington. She wiped her eyes and turned to her.

"Mrs. McPhail is my guardian . . . and my aunt. Well, a sort of aunt. She was my father's half-sister. She works me hard because . . . I guess because she feels entitled to." Briefly she told the story of how she and John had been left orphans after the fire, of the Wilburs, of Mrs. McPhail's coming and then Mr. Blackwood's, of her father's will, of coming to York.

"And that farm, you see, the farm where we lived when my parents were alive, is the one that Mr. Blackwood bought and, I guess, is now trying to sell to you and Major Heatherington." Emma clutched her hands together in an anguished movement and looked at Mrs. Heatherington. "And I've been so worried about what to do. You see, Mr. Blackwood wasn't telling you the truth about the farm. He was making it sound better than it is. Though it really is quite a good farm, and the Wilburs across the road are nice neighbors. I wish you could have met Granny Wilbur but she's dead now."

Abruptly Emma began crying again. Without thinking, forgetting the distance that should separate hotel guests and servants, she flung herself on the pillows of the Heatheringtons' bed and wept aloud.

Mrs. Heatherington shifted to the chair and put one arm across Emma's shoulders. "Oh, my dear, what a lot of sadness and worry for you."

"And of course Mrs. McPhail is not very motherly," Emma mumbled. "She wanted servants, not children. She pays me wages, but I can't talk to her about . . . about anything."

"No, I can see that."

Emma forced herself to sit up but was still sobbing and blowing her nose when Major Heatherington and Caroline came in. She was about to bolt for the attic when Mrs.

Heatherington, holding on to Emma, firmly ordered Caroline to go to her room and close the door. Apparently this was done because a moment later, when Emma emerged from behind the handkerchief, the only other person in the room was the Major, looking at his wife with a puzzled and worried face.

"Did you know that poor Emma is Mrs. McPhail's niece?" Mrs. Heatherington asked him, "and that she has to work like a navvy?"

"It's not always this bad," Emma managed to say, "only now when . . ."

"And that it's Emma's family's farm that Mr. Blackwood is trying to sell? Sit down, Charles, we must talk about this. But first find us a dry handkerchief, if you please. One of your large ones."

It took the Major a moment's rummaging but he did produce one.

"And two glasses of madeira, please, Charles. Emma is completely overwrought. Would you like some madeira, child?"

"I've never had madeira . . . but . . . yes, please. Just a little."

The Major set down a full and a half glass of wine on the bedside table, poured a third glass for himself, and pulled up a chair. "Well, now, what is this all about?"

Mrs. Heatherington briefly told the story and Emma, taking a sip of madeira and trying to become calm, marveled that she had so clearly grasped the essentials of what Emma had related in a very muddled way.

"You see how this concerns us, Charles."

"Yes, of course. I'm glad Emma didn't wait any longer to tell us." He looked at her gravely but didn't express his reproach any further.

"I was trying to decide whether, if I told you, I would be disloyal to Mrs. McPhail and Mr. Blackwood."

"Surely you don't owe Blackwood anything," he said.

"No, but he and Mrs. McPhail probably work together."

"So that your aunt will receive a portion of Blackwood's profit on the farm."

Emma remembered the evening when she had overheard Mrs. McPhail and Mr. Blackwood talking – how happy she had been at the thought of the Heatheringtons living on the farm and how angry when she guessed what might actually be going on.

"I . . . I had thought she might. Would it be possible?"

"Oh, yes, very easily."

They compared the price that Blackwood had paid for the farm with what he was now asking. "He'd make three hundred dollars clear profit," said the Major musingly. "In the space of a few weeks. And your aunt would, if my guess is right, get some of it."

Emma sipped her wine, which she was enjoying.

"Well, I'm glad we have not committed ourselves yet. Tell us something about the farm, Emma." He leaned back and picked up his glass.

Emma did so, trying to deal with both the good and bad features, the wild-grape vines on their sunny slope and the gloom of the bush, the well-built shanty as well as the burned ruin of the house.

"How big would you say the cottage is . . . or rather the shanty, as you call it?" the Major asked.

She looked around. "Smaller than this room. Maybe the same length but slightly narrower." She gestured with the bandaged hand.

The Heatheringtons looked too, and their faces became rather long. "And that's all there is? Only one room?" he asked. "Not even an attic?"

"That's all," said Emma, "but it keeps the weather out, and it has a wooden floor and a proper fireplace with a chimney. Some shanties have a dirt floor and just a hole to let the smoke out. We lived in ours – Mother and Father, with me as baby, and then John – for five years before the house was built."

Nobody spoke for a few moments. Emma had time to realize again that the information she had given might turn the Heatheringtons against the farm – that she might have defeated her own hope of their buying it – and that if Mrs. McPhail heard of this (as she almost certainly would) she'd be very angry at Emma.

"I had not expected this of Blackwood," said the Major sadly. "I thought him honest."

"Perhaps he is only mistaken," Mrs. Heatherington said in a consoling, encouraging voice.

Emma could not let that pass. "He saw the farm," she said. "He rode all over the cleared parts and had a good look at the barn and the shanty. Mrs. McPhail actually lived in the shanty for more than a week."

The Major sighed. "Well, I don't like admitting that I was wrong about a man but I see that I must."

Emma brought up a matter that was worrying her. "I guess you'll have to tell Mr. Blackwood that I was the one who . . . who . . ."

The Major looked at her soberly for a moment. "I can see your difficulty. You feel that you've been dishonorable in speaking to us behind your aunt's back."

Emma blushed and looked down at her bandaged hand.

"But consider our side, Emma. We have to go to Blackwood and say that we cannot continue negotiating on the former basis because we've received new information about the farm. I think he will guess very easily from whom that information came. Or we must tell him that we are no longer interested in this piece of land and begin all over again with some other dealer."

"Yes, I see."

Then suddenly she had an idea. "Suppose you inspected the farm for yourself? You could go there now that the weather is good. Just tell Mr. Blackwood that you'd like to take advantage of the fine weather to go and see the place. You could ride. We came here by wagon, which was very slow, but if you hired a riding horse . . ."

Mrs. Heatherington frowned. "Isn't it a great distance? And after all, we now have a more reliable description of the farm."

The Major considered the matter at greater length. "No," he said at last, "I must see it for myself. Going to Blackwood with only Emma's description would put me in a weak bargaining position. And of course I'd much prefer not to have to mention Emma at all. So I must inspect the farm myself."

"Yes, of course, I see that now," his wife said quickly. "*We* must inspect it – because I'll go with you. But it is rather far, and we hear such dreadful things of the roads outside town." She glanced at Emma and then turned back to the Major.

He looked more hopeful. "I met a man last week who lives in Thornhill, about fourteen miles north of here, and it takes him between two and three hours to make the journey. This farm of Blackwood's is forty miles away – or probably rather more, if he was misleading us about that too."

"The road is not very good," Emma admitted. "But there are inns along the way. As far as Waterdown you take the Dundas Road that Governor Simcoe built." She was proud of remembering this from her father's lessons.

"The man in Thornhill travels about six miles an hour," the Major calculated. "We might do five. That would mean reaching the farm in a long day's riding, if we left early in the morning. We'd need a couple of hours there and then we'd ride back. Two very long days might be sufficient – except that it is dark early in the evenings now. Probably we would be wise to break the return trip." He turned to Emma. "Is this fine weather likely to last?"

"It's hard to be sure. This is what we call Indian summer, and it can last several days or even a week. It doesn't *feel* as though it's going to change soon – there's no wind, none of that restless feeling in the air. But of course if it ended suddenly you'd have rain and mud."

"What about snow?"

"We don't often have snow in October but if there is any it's wet, and that still means muddy roads."

Mrs. Heatherington smiled. "Don't look so worried, Emma. We can cope with mud. It will slow us down but not stop us. We'd better set out tomorrow, Charles, and hope that the good weather lasts for a few more days."

Suddenly she frowned; her eyes met her husband's and then shifted expressively to the door of their daughter's room. The meaning was clear: they would have to decide whether to take Caroline along or whether one of them should stay behind with her.

"We'll have to think about that," Mrs. Heatherington said. "In the meantime, I'm sure Emma is longing for her bed."

"Of course," said Emma, recognizing dismissal. "Thank you for looking after my hand."

"Thank you for your information. If things are made difficult for you, be sure to tell us. We wouldn't want you to be punished for helping us."

"I will." Quickly, without stopping to think, she lightly kissed Mrs. Heatherington's cheek and then hurried from the room.

TEN

Caroline

As often happened now, Emma woke the next morning before Mrs. Jones came in. Immediately she remembered that something momentous had happened. She had spoken with the Heatheringtons, given them the information they needed, started them on a different course of action. She had also given them cause to mistrust Mr. Blackwood.

In doing all this, she had solved one problem. But she had created another, that of keeping Mrs. McPhail from learning what she had done. Emma was fairly sure, however, that her aunt would find this out eventually; she seemed to have an instinct for such things. She would be very angry, with the cold and restrained anger that Emma dreaded. And when that happened, could Emma really count on the Heatheringtons' support?

As she dressed, the bandage on her hand making her clumsy, she realized that Mrs. McPhail would also be annoyed at Emma and Mrs. Tubb for having hurt themselves.

Before going downstairs, she had a few words with John, explaining what had happened the evening before. She stressed the danger of Mr. Blackwood or Mrs. McPhail learning of it. "So don't show them that we know about the Heatheringtons being interested in our farm."

Then she asked him if he could lend her a dollar. After the fire, the Wilburs had bought some fabric from the peddler for her to make underwear, and this was her chance to repay them.

"Sure I'll lend you a dollar," he said with the offhand generosity of the newly rich man. He went to a dark corner where the bare roof rafters met the floor and after a moment's fumbling came back with a knotted piece of cloth. Under Emma's fascinated gaze he untied it and counted out a dollar in small coins, thereby almost exhausting his hoard.

"I'll find something to tie it up in," she said as she took the money, "and ask Mrs. Heatherington to take it along." She would also have liked to write a letter to the Wilburs but without writing materials did not know how.

The problem about the letter was solved, however, when Emma went upstairs after breakfast to do the bedrooms. Mrs. Heatherington was in her room packing a cloth bag with a few things for herself and her husband. She had the door ajar and beckoned Emma to come in.

"I thought you might like to write a note for me to take to your friends," she said. "Or I could carry a message."

"I *would* like to write a note," Emma said, "but I have nothing to write with."

"You're welcome to use our things," Mrs. Heatherington said, gesturing at the table on which stood a portable writing desk with ink, pen, and paper ready for use.

"Oh!" Emma exclaimed, pleased at the forethought. "But I can't take long. I'm suppose to be doing the rooms."

"A few minutes will make no difference. You can say that the bandage on your hand slowed you down. How does the hand feel this morning?"

"It's throbbing a bit but that's all," Emma said as she sat down at the table.

"If it begins to hurt while I'm away, be sure to have someone look at it."

"I'll ask Mrs. Jones, the cook. She looks after us when we're hurt or sick."

While Emma wrote, Mrs. Heatherington finished her packing and left the room. She came back while Emma was sprinkling sand on the completed letter to dry the ink.

"That's done? Good."

"Would you mind also taking a small package for Mr. and Mrs. Wilbur? It's money – a dollar that I borrowed in the spring and would like to repay." She took the little bundle from her pocket and held it out.

"I'll be happy to."

Mrs. Heatherington tucked the letter and the money into a corner of the cloth bag. Then she sat down on the bed facing Emma. "I've just had a word with Mrs. McPhail. Of course I had to tell her that my husband and I would be away for two or three days. I simply said that the good weather gave us an opportunity to go and see the farm for ourselves. She knew all about the business because it was she who originally put us in touch with Mr. Blackwood. I asked whether she – and Miss Morgan, who happened to be present – would keep an eye on Caroline, who is staying here."

Emma thought with misgivings of Caroline's willful behavior, but she said nothing.

"The Major and I decided after you left us last night that there is no reason whatsoever for Mrs. McPhail or Mr. Blackwood to know that you told us anything. So you may be easy about that." She smiled and stood up. "And now perhaps you had better get on with your usual work."

"Thank you . . . for everything, Mrs. Heatherington."

"It was a pleasure, Emma. You did us an important service."

Soon after that the travelers departed and the hotel was quiet except for a lady guest who was making a great fuss about having seen a mouse in her room. Mrs. McPhail was handling the affair in her usual adroit way, doing everything possible to solve the problem and placate the guest but without being subservient. Emma, finishing the bedrooms while this affair was in full swing, again found herself respecting her aunt's abilities and wondering that one person could be such a mixture of admirable and unlovable traits.

Emma's main concern that day was with the weather. It was another warm, hazy, Indian-summer day; she fervently hoped that there would be no change until the Heatheringtons returned from their trip.

Because it was Sunday, she was excused from working on the apples but did have to go to church in the afternoon. Immediately after the service John went off with another boy – exploring, they said. Emma walked home past the

Anchor but the sound of rowdy laughter from inside made
her unwilling to go in by herself.

Back at the hotel, Mrs. Jones made her a hot drink and
advised her to go and have a rest. After washing the handkerchiefs and other cloths she had used that morning – being
careful, as she had been all day, to keep the bandage on her
hand dry – and hanging them from the edges of the shelves in
her room, Emma drank Mrs. Jones' potion and lay down on
her bed.

She reached to the shelf above the bed and took down the
first volume of *Pamela*. Already in the twenty or thirty pages
that Emma had read, the servant girl Pamela had been
assailed by the indecent demands of her master. He had even
given her beautiful clothes! Emma was eager to find out how
all this would work out – though when she stopped to think
she was surprised that in Pamela's life there was so little
drudgery and so much time for writing the letters to her
parents by means of which the story was told.

But before she had read more than a couple of pages, Emma
dozed off. She was eventually awakened by the buzzing of a
wasp, which had come in through the open window.

After shooing the insect out, Emma stayed at the window
for a moment, looking out and listening. Not a breath of air
stirred; in the gardens below her, yellow leaves fell straight
down from the branches of the fruit trees. Someone was
sawing wood, people were talking, far away a piano was being
played. A horse's hooves thudded on the dusty road.

Her eyes moved to the far ridge of land, the autumn colors
of which were dulled to rust by the haze. Suddenly she wished
she were there, walking among the trees over the springy
layer of fallen leaves and pine needles, watching squirrels

dashing about their autumnal business and listening to the savage shriek of the blue jays. She recalled days like this when she had gone with her mother into the woods to gather kindling for the winter's fires.

Abruptly she sneezed and then, after blowing her nose, she smiled to herself, aware that she was remembering her mother now with a good deal of pleasure as well as sorrow. The memories of her parents were as vivid as ever but they were becoming less painful, more sustaining.

Emma returned to her reading until the clock downstairs struck five, which meant that it was nearly time to go and help prepare dinner. She tidied her hair and, after chasing out another wasp, closed the window. Mrs. McPhail was adamant about closing windows against the night air.

Mrs. Jones was in the kitchen but not making a big bustle about supper. The Indian-summer languor, combined with that of Sunday afternoon, seemed to affect everything. "Cold chicken they're getting, and fish pie, and pickles. Oh, and Mrs. McPhail says there's no candles in the drawer in the parlor dresser and new ones needed in the sconces in the lobby."

Emma took a large handful of candles from the box in the larder and went through the kitchen into the guests' parlor where she deposited all but two of them in the drawer of the dresser. No one was in the room, but through the open window she could hear quiet voices from the veranda. There was a wasp in the room; before dinner someone should catch it but as long as the windows were open it would be a waste of time.

The two remaining candles she took with her to the lobby, where they would be put in the sconces. These were simple wooden brackets with metal reflectors and dishes to catch the molten wax. She lifted them down off their hooks and set them on the counter, making a mental note that they would have to be properly cleaned soon, the old wax scraped out of the sockets and the metal parts washed in hot water to remove the scattered spots of wax. But for now she would just push the new candles in among the ruins of the old ones.

As she was doing this she heard Mrs. McPhail's voice. The door to her room was closed but presumably the sound came through open windows. ". . . farm . . ." Mrs. McPhail said, and then after some indistinguishable words, ". . . they can reasonably quarrel with."

"I took him for a softy, one of those noble types," Mr. Blackwood said in a slightly irritated tone. "I suppose his wife put him up to this."

"Of course we may have to come down from the six hundred dollars."

"It's not an unfair price. A bit high but not outrageous. Quite an area cleared. Why, a house in town would cost him seven hundred and fifty."

"A *house*. The farm has only what you so blithely call a cottage."

"The Major's own word." There was a pause. Emma made no haste in fixing and straightening the candles. "It's understood that we still split the profit evenly, Harriet, whatever it is. This . . . this inspection of theirs is not my fault."

Emma, hanging up a candle sconce and making sure that it hung straight, held her breath to hear more. But the only sounds audible now were the clinkings of teacups. It appeared that her responsibility for the Heatheringtons' trip to see the farm was not suspected – indeed, if it had been, she would surely have been questioned or scolded before now.

Equally important was the confirmation of her guess that

the two would share the profit made from the resale of the farm, and the fact that the selling price was rather high. Had this been news to her, she would have been very angry and indignant, but now her main reaction was a bleak relief at having been right.

But she was astonished and appalled at the cosy, domestic tone of the discussion. What scoundrels those two were, chatting in an almost desultory way over their Sunday afternoon cups of tea about a deal to cheat two orphans and a pair of harmless immigrants. Nothing in their tone even suggested that they were trying to be secretive about it.

The weather was still fair the following day. The Heatheringtons would probably reach the farm sometime this morning, Emma had calculated, and might begin their return journey this afternoon or tomorrow.

After breakfast she came across Caroline trying to borrow money from Miss Morgan. "It's absurd!" the girl exclaimed in a high, tense voice. "They left me only a few pence!"

Emma gave a quick glance at both of them, wondering whether Miss Morgan would lend the money.

"Come upstairs with me, Miss Heatherington," the lady said.

That evening Caroline did not appear at the hotel for dinner. Mrs. McPhail was not there either – Mrs. Delaney presided over the table in her stead – and Emma saw that Miss Morgan was uneasy. That lady had seated herself at the end of the table usually occupied by the Heatheringtons, obviously to be near Caroline, and there she sat in solitude, eating little but fidgeting with her knife and fork.

After the meal, she asked Mrs. Delaney when Mrs. McPhail might be expected home.

"She's seeing about some immigrants, but she said she wouldn't be late."

Miss Morgan stood still for a moment. She was so absorbed with her thoughts that she did not notice the difficulty that Emma was having in maneuvering past her with a tray of dirty dishes. When the tray accidentally bumped her elbow, she came to herself with a start.

"I'll be here in the parlor," she said to Mrs. Delaney and Emma. "I would like to see Miss Heatherington and Mrs. McPhail when they come in."

She went to her room to get her embroidery and then established herself downstairs in the parlor with the door slightly ajar. She ordered tea. Emma, when she brought it, wondered whether Miss Morgan knew about Caroline's usual carryings-on and whether the knowledge of them would make Miss Morgan more worried or less.

In Emma's presence, apparently, Miss Morgan felt obliged to hide her real concern a bit. "That girl!" she said with a little laugh. "If I were her mother I know how I'd deal with her."

"She seems to like to have her own way," Emma commented, wishing that she could help Miss Morgan somehow.

"Pampered, that's what she is!" exploded Miss Morgan, forgetting to dissemble. "When I have girls in my charge I'll keep them in order." She poured herself a cup of tea. "And I'll need another candle, Emma. I can't see what I'm doing. I should remember not to start such fine work at the beginning of the winter."

When Emma had brought the second candlestick and was returning to the kitchen, Mrs. McPhail arrived. Miss Morgan, hearing her, came to the parlor door.

"Oh, I'm glad you're back, Mrs. McPhail. Miss Heatherington did not come home for dinner and is not back yet. Nearly nine o'clock!" she said, gesturing at the clock in the lobby.

Mrs. McPhail was still for a moment. Her face was smooth but had a curious intentness that suggested to Emma that the news was even more alarming than it had seemed. Emma shivered; as Mrs. McPhail and Miss Morgan went to the parlor and shut the door, she returned to the kitchen and warmed herself at the low fire. But after that, feeling uneasy, she opened the back door and stood for a moment in the yard. A filmy cloud half concealed the moon, and there was no wind stirring the warm air. It might have been called a fine night but to Emma it felt indefinably strange.

A few minutes later, as Emma was filling a jug of water to take up to her bedroom, Mrs. McPhail came into the kitchen. "I suppose you're aware that Miss Heatherington has not come in," she said. Mrs. Jones, Emma, John, and young Joe Tubb all looked up.

"Dear, dear," said Mrs. Jones.

"Do any of you happen to know what she was planning to do today? Or did you boys see her about when you were in town? It would be a great help to know whom she was with."

"No, ma'am," they both said.

"I believe she spends most of her time with the officers, especially Captain Dixon and . . . and a Captain Marshall," said Emma. "And with one of the officers' wives, but I don't know which one."

"Yes, I'd heard that too. I want you, Joe, to take a message to the commander of the fort."

"Now?"

"Yes. Wait here – I'll write it and bring it out to you. Be sure you carry a lantern."

"It's moonlight."

"All the same, if you go without a lantern someone may take you for a footpad."

Joe yawned and grumbled inarticulately but lit the lantern and put on his coat.

Mrs. McPhail was back a few minutes later. "There you are," she said, giving Joe a sealed note. "Take it to the officers' barracks in the fort and give it to the officer in charge. Wait for an answer. When you return, come to the front door and give the reply to me. Is that clear?"

When Joe was gone, Mrs. McPhail turned to Mrs. Jones. "You and Emma may go to bed, Mrs. Jones. You'll lock up, of course. I'll let Joe in when he returns." At the doorway she turned and came back. "I think I'll take a kettle of water to heat over the parlor fire so that Miss Morgan and I can have some fresh tea later."

"You'll be sitting up then, ma'am?"

"Until the young lady returns. Good night."

As Emma undressed, she alternated between thinking that the situation was not serious – that Caroline would come home any minute now – and that it might be very serious indeed. Could she have taken the opportunity of her parents' absence to elope? Could she have come to some harm?

Through her mind flickered disturbing images connected with Henrietta Street. But she pushed them aside – they were too lurid and did not fit at all with Miss Caroline Heatherington.

ELEVEN

An Uncomfortable Errand

The next morning, when Emma went to the parlor with her broom and dusters, Miss Morgan was there standing and staring out of a window at the darkness.

"She hasn't come?" Emma asked.

Miss Morgan turned away from the window. Her face was extremely tired and grave, marked with lines and shadows. She had a shawl pulled tightly around her, though the fire had apparently been kept stoked all night. "No. I don't know how I will be able to tell her parents."

"Major and Mrs. Heatherington will probably not be back until late this afternoon or even tomorrow. Miss Heatherington may return when it's daylight."

"She may," said Miss Morgan grimly. "But in what condition? . . ."

"You're expecting something really serious?"

"One always does, at times like this." Miss Morgan covered her face with both hands for a moment, then dropped them and shook her head. "Even if she returns – and no matter in what condition – I will have failed in my charge. My hopes of setting up a school are over. No one in York will trust me after this."

"Oh, Miss Morgan!" Emma had not thought of this; she lifted her hands in a gesture of protest.

"No, I'm not exaggerating. I was trusted by the parents to look after this girl and I failed. Will people give their daughters into my care in the future?"

Emma said nothing, fearing that Miss Morgan might be right. After a moment, rather apologetically, she began to sweep the hearth; the hotel's operations could not be further upset, and there were other guests to be considered. She was just wondering whether she would have to clean around Miss Morgan when that lady said, "I think I'll go to my room and freshen up."

"I'll tell Mrs. Tubb to bring you your hot water."

For the rest of the morning a hush of anxiety hung over the hotel. Mrs. McPhail went out to see people who might know something or be able to help, and Miss Morgan stayed home to receive Caroline if she returned. Emma hesitantly asked Mrs. Delaney whether she had told what she knew about Caroline's doings – nosiness had its uses at a time like this – and was told that she had talked to Mrs. McPhail on the previous evening.

Then, just before lunch, a few minutes after Mrs. McPhail had returned with a grim face from her futile quest, a carriage drew up at the door and out of it stepped Caroline accompanied by an officer and lady whom Emma had never seen before. They hurried into the hotel and were immediately taken by Miss Morgan into Mrs. McPhail's room.

Emma was beginning to think that she would never hear what had happened when, later in the afternoon, Miss Morgan stopped her in the lobby. She was still grave. "You have been so concerned about this business, Emma, that I thought you had a right to know what occurred. Miss Heatherington, together with Captain Dixon and some other people, went out on the lake in a sailboat yesterday and were becalmed far from shore. They were forced to stay out there all night."

"Couldn't they have rowed back?"

"It seems there were no oars in the boat."

"I hope she has not taken cold again?"

"There's no sign of cold or ague yet but she has gone straight to bed. And she will be confined within these four walls until her parents return."

"Well, at least no one can blame you for this, Miss Morgan."

"People can and will blame me. We'll hope that there are no unpleasant consequences."

Caroline kept to her bed until late afternoon. Then she dressed and began restlessly wandering about the hotel, up the stairs and down, into the guests' parlor and across the lobby and upstairs again. When Emma went to tidy herself before dinner, Caroline followed her and caught up with her in the attic.

"Yes, Miss Heatherington? Did you want something?"

Caroline glanced quickly around, then came close to Emma. She was shorter and plumper than Emma and today her face was without its usual healthy color.

"You must run an errand for me."

"I will be busy until about nine o'clock this evening. But Joe . . ."

"No, I want you to do it. After nine o'clock will do very well."

Emma was about to refuse but she sensed the tension and anxiety in the girl. Sympathy, and a bit of curiosity, kept her silent but attentive.

"I'll pay you," Caroline said.

"What is the errand?"

"Last night in the boat Captain Dixon challenged Captain Marshall."

"Challenged?"

"To a duel."

"Duels are illegal," Emma said, having learned that from Mrs. Jones.

Caroline shrugged. "They're fought secretly though. One took place just this summer, in the woods. It was called a hunting accident. And even if they are illegal, ordinary fighting is not." She walked away a few steps, then turned to face Emma. "Mind you, it would be something of an honor to have gentlemen fight a duel over one, but at this moment I don't think . . . I'd rather no one were hurt. So I'd like to stop the fight or duel or whatever it is. Nothing can happen until tonight because I believe Captain Dixon is on duty until ten o'clock."

"But what do you want me to do?"

"Carry messages to them. Look, I've already written the notes." She took two notes from her pocket and held them up, their red wax seals plainly visible. "I've printed the names in large letters. Can you read?" She came close to Emma again and held out the letters separately, one in each hand. "This one is for Captain Marshall and this . . ."

"Thank you, I can read," Emma said rather curtly.

"Well, then, all you have to do is go to the officers' mess – that's in the fort – and deliver these notes. The gentlemen will certainly be there – I heard them say so last night. I'll pay you ten cents, five now and five when you return. Come to my room when you've done it and tell me what happened, if anything did, or what they said. *Please*, Emma. Of course I'd go myself but I'm imprisoned here and I'm very anxious to prevent their fighting and maybe killing each other. You must help me – there's no one else who will."

By now Caroline was looking extremely anguished and entreating. Emma was not impressed by the dramatics but it seemed to her that under the exaggerated words and manner the girl was genuinely worried. Even if she had been the cause of this impending fight, she now seemed determined to prevent it. Her motive might be selfish – she could not afford any more black marks against her at present – but the intention itself was still a good one.

Emma took a much graver view of dueling or any kind of fighting than Caroline did. People were often maimed for life, even killed. Eyes were blinded, teeth knocked out, bones broken. In the kitchen she had heard such things mentioned; her father and Joseph Tubb were examples of men whose whole lives had been affected by injuries. She had wondered sometimes if her father's weak arm, hurt during the war with the Americans, might not have contributed to his failure to help his wife and babies escape the burning house. So she was ready to help in an attempt to prevent a fight.

Nevertheless it was with considerable misgivings that she agreed to carry the messages, mainly because it was to be done without the knowledge of Miss Morgan and Mrs. McPhail, whom Caroline bitterly called "the watchdogs."

While putting on her cloak that evening, Emma wondered about taking the lantern. She remembered what her aunt had said to Joe the evening before: a lantern was a sign that a person walking outdoors at night was on legitimate business. But the lantern hung in plain view near the back door. If she took it, its absence (and her own) would almost certainly be noticed. So it was without a light that she slipped out the back door, through the yard, and into the street.

A nearly full yellowish moon shone but occasional clouds slid over it. Emma hoped that for the next hour there would be more moonlight and fewer clouds. They and the restless, gusty wind suggested that the weather might be about to change. That would mean rain and muddy roads for the Heatheringtons.

She had never been to the fort but John had told her where it was. So had her father, who had been stationed there when he was a young man in the army. To reach it she had only to walk down to Front Street, the road that ran along the shore of the lake, turn right, and keep walking westward. She hurried along, wanting to finish this errand and go to bed no later than necessary – and reflecting rather resentfully that Caroline didn't have to get up at five o'clock in the morning.

But after the first few minutes she found herself enjoying the trip, especially when she reached Front Street. There she turned west and walked with the lake on her left and the big houses and gardens of important people on her right. The moonlight touched the water with bright spots and the wind made small waves rustle on the shore beyond the low bluffs. The houses showed lights, visible among the bare trees, and in one there seemed to be a party in progress because all the windows were lit and several carriages were drawn up on the sweeping driveway in front. Emma could hear nothing from inside the house, but a murmur and a sudden laugh came from the waiting coachmen.

When the row of houses ended, though, she became apprehensive. The road was empty before her. To the right stood a tavern with an unreadable sign; she heard the drinkers' noisy talk as she hurried by. Just then, too, a large cloud obscured the moon and the wind tugged at her cloak.

She walked on, stumbling once or twice, and was glad when the moon reappeared. By its light she discovered that the fort was just ahead. She could see open gates in the surrounding wall. Beyond were buildings and lights, for all the world like another small town.

Emma paused in the gateway. There was a sentry box but no one challenged her. In fact, she was confronted by the unmilitary sight of a woman leading a small child by the hand and carrying a bucket. Somewhere a baby was crying.

Several buildings were clustered nearby, all with lights on. She wondered how she could find out which was the officers' barracks. Although there were signs of activity – shadowy figures moving across windows, voices raised – there was no one visible once the woman with the child had gone.

She recognized the blockhouse from her father's description and, thinking that that must surely be a place of some authority, began to walk toward it. But just then two soldiers appeared, strolling idly in her direction.

"Excuse me," she said.

"Evening, ma'am."

"I'm looking for the officers' barracks. Can you tell me where they are?"

"Straight ahead, ma'am, last building to the right."

"Thank you."

She hurried on. Through a briefly opened door in one building she saw men playing cards; on a stoop someone sat smoking. Laundry hung from lines, and firewood was piled against walls.

She reached the indicated building and knocked on the door but there were raised voices inside and she was afraid that no one had heard her. She knocked twice more and then hesitantly opened the door and went in. She found herself in a small vestibule beyond, which was a large room with a long central table, a number of lit candles, and probably twenty men. Four of them were playing cards at a distant smaller table, but the rest were gathered in the center of the room watching or participating in a conversation going on there.

A tall clock against the far wall showed the time to be a few minutes before ten, the time when, according to Caroline, Captain Dixon came off duty. The girls had decided that Emma would wait out of sight until he arrived and then hand the notes to him and Captain Marshall. So Emma prepared to wait in the shadows of the vestibule, standing where she could watch the room and also the door by which she had just entered. She was sure that she would recognize him because he had dined several times at the hotel.

While waiting, she looked to see whether Captain Marshall was in the room. But she had seen him only once, on the street, when she was too agitated to form a clear picture.

Besides, the men in the room were closely grouped together and the flickering candlelight on their white shirts made them all look much alike.

Suddenly the tone of the talk changed. There was a shout and one man flung the contents of a wineglass at another. Men jumped to their feet, moved chairs aside, lifted candles. In the scattering, Emma caught sight of Captain Dixon. Caroline had been wrong! He was here already!

"By God, Marshall," he exclaimed, wiping wine off his face with one sweep of his sleeve, "I won't stand for this!"

"Stand for what?" demanded the other officer, who was still lounging in a chair in the middle of the shifting crowd.

Emma took a few steps forward, hoping that she might yet avert the fight by delivering the notes. But how was she to get through the swirling crowd of officers moving chairs and wine bottles?

Then she was pushed aside by two or three more men who had rushed in through the door behind her and were eagerly joining the excitement.

The argument was still going on.

"You've been poaching for a month now. I'll put an end to it."

"How?"

"A friend of mine will wait on you. . . ."

"No dueling!" cried several voices, and one man laughed.

In an instant, before Emma could move a foot further or raise a cry, the fight was on. Fists swung and two bodies hit the floor with a crash that jolted the whole building and made the candle flames shake. The cardplayers, after one disgusted glance at what was happening, picked up their cards and wineglasses and left the room by the far door.

To Emma, standing aghast and speechless, it looked as though no one could survive such a fight. The two men were on their feet again, battering each other. A fist hit a face and left it bloody. One man – Emma could no longer tell them apart – nearly choked his opponent by gripping and twisting his shirt collar. A shiny boot caught the other man's leg and both plunged to the floor again.

The bystanders, perched on the furniture or holding candles up to provide more light, noisily commented and cheered; one punched the air and then rapidly drank a whole glass of wine.

All of a sudden there was a hiss of warning and then silence. In the far doorway stood a stern-looking older man, clearly a superior officer.

"Stop it, damn you. Stop at once. Someone fetch the surgeon."

The fighters, on the floor in a heap, were still for a moment. Then Marshall got to his knees and shook his head back and forth. He used loose shreds of his torn shirt to wipe the blood off his face. In a moment he pulled himself up onto a chair.

Dixon was stirring slightly. One of the bystanders went to squat beside him, lifting him into a half-sitting position and holding him there. One arm lay as if it were dead. Though his face was bloody, he made no effort to wipe it.

"I suppose you're quarreling over that girl again," said the senior officer. When no one replied, he added, "In the morning, if you aren't in your coffins, I'll see you both."

The bystanders began dispersing, talking in undertones but in an amused and excited way. Emma stayed where she was, realizing that it was futile now to deliver the notes that might have averted the fight but feeling all the same that taking them back to Caroline would be even more pointless. So when most of the men had gone she darted forward and laid the notes down close to the hurt officers. She was not sure that anyone saw them but perhaps they would later. Caroline had said that there would be no replies.

Then, reflecting grimly on such useless and destructive fighting and on the other men's enjoyment of it, she set off for home.

By now the wind was colder and the moon almost permanently hidden behind clouds. Emma was very sorry not to have taken the lantern. Several times she nearly tripped. As she passed the tavern outside the gates, a noisy group of men came out and turned toward the fort. She stayed out of their way. A moment later two silent men emerged and headed for the town, walking a short distance behind her. That frightened her. She was tempted to run but knew that that might provoke them – and besides, if she tried to run she would almost certainly trip and fall.

The two men came no closer, however, and gradually her heart hammered a little less fiercely. Further on, after she had turned off Front Street to go north, she was more annoyed than frightened by a drunken man hurtling out of a tavern doorway and falling in a heap at her feet.

When she was back in the hotel she took her candle and went silently – and, she hoped, unseen – to report to Caroline.

At the top of the first flight she stopped. The door of the Heatheringtons' room was partly open; through the gap she could see Miss Morgan sitting in a chair reading. This was unexpected. As Emma was still wondering what to do next, Miss Morgan looked up and saw her. She put her book down and came toward Emma; at the same time Caroline, still fully dressed, came out of her room.

"Are you looking for Miss Heatherington?" Miss Morgan asked Emma in a chilling voice.

Emma glanced at Caroline for help. She knew that her errand should be kept secret from Miss Morgan but could not invent another explanation for being there so late and still in her cloak.

Receiving no answer, Miss Morgan turned to Caroline. "Well, Miss Heatherington? I presume you are behind this, whatever it is. If you don't want Emma to be scolded, you'd better tell me."

It looked as though Caroline would refuse. She tossed her head and made rather a poor pretence of sobbing into a wisp of a handkerchief pulled out of the bosom of her dress. But Miss Morgan waited calmly, and eventually Caroline explained about the fight and the urgent need to send messages to the two officers concerned.

"I *must* know what happened," she said with an elaborate pleading look at Miss Morgan. "Will you let me ask Emma?"

"Certainly. I would like to know myself what happened."

Emma reported, seeing it all in her mind and again becoming angry at such senseless violence and injury.

"They were both hurt?" Caroline asked with what looked like a mixture of concern and excitement.

"Yes. Rather badly, I thought."

"But they were sitting up?"

"Captain Dixon had to be helped."

Caroline stared at nothing for a few moments. "Because of me," she said at last with a sigh that might have been one of regret at the violence or pleasure at the gentlemen's valor.

Miss Morgan sent both girls to bed. "And don't close your door, Miss Heatherington. I insist on being able to see you from my chair."

When Emma paused at the foot of the attic stair to look back, she saw Miss Morgan taking up her book again.

It was not until she was in bed that she remembered the five cents that Caroline had promised to pay her when she returned.

TWELVE

Several Truths

The following morning was cold and rainy. The chill seemed to have penetrated to every corner of the building, even to the kitchen, where the fire had sunk deep under the ashes used to bank it.

During breakfast Mrs. McPhail said, in reply to a question of Miss Morgan's, that the Heatheringtons should be back at any time.

Miss Morgan had brought her embroidery down to the parlor and after breakfast she settled herself by the fire, insisting that Caroline stay in the room with her. Calmly she disregarded the girl's restless fidgeting over some sewing, a book that she wasn't reading, and a letter that she couldn't seem to begin writing. At lunch Caroline ate almost nothing and afterward, with heavy sarcasm to dramatize her imprisonment, asked for permission to lie down for a rest. Miss Morgan granted it but posted herself in the Heatheringtons' room, doggedly embroidering.

A bit later, Emma was in the attic, putting apples for winter preservation in their bed of dry sand, when there was a clatter on the stairs and Caroline appeared, staring about her frantically.

"Are you looking for something?" Emma asked.

"They've come back! I don't want to see them!"

"Your parents? You'll have to see them sooner or later."

"The watchdogs will tell them horrid things and they'll hate me."

"Mrs. McPhail and Miss Morgan will have to report, of course. But are your parents so strict with you?" Emma knew that she was not being very kind but she had little sympathy with this girl's exaggerated airs and moods. Being becalmed out on the lake might not have been her fault but she couldn't be so easily excused for her sauciness to her parents and her apparent responsibility for the fight at the officers' mess.

Caroline was wandering around the attic now, no longer frantic but clearly postponing the confrontation. She hadn't answered Emma's question about her parents' strictness.

"I like attics, don't you?" she said, tracing the curved back of an old chair and then blowing the dust off her finger. She paused for a moment to stare down at John's pallet on the floor and then moved on.

"This is the first one I've ever known," said Emma, resuming her work on the apples. "The first one like this, I mean, with old furniture stored in it. At home the attic was where everybody slept – just one big bedroom."

"Well, of course, servants always sleep in the attic."

Emma stiffened and turned to face the other girl. "I'm only a servant by necessity, Miss Heatherington. I'm as wellborn as you. I'm also a gentleman's daughter. My parents, who are both dead now, were not servants."

"Oh, really? How very interesting!" But her tone was indifferent and she gave less attention to Emma than to a storage chest whose lid she had lifted in idle curiosity. "Empty," she remarked, dropping the lid with a bang and wiping her fingers on a tiny handkerchief. "Well, these things happen, don't they? People die. I suppose I'd better see them – *my* parents – and find out what they have to say."

Without a further look at Emma, she went downstairs.

Emma, her fist pressed against her mouth, stared after her. The attic seemed to echo with Caroline's words: "Oh, really? . . . these things happen . . . these things happen . . . people die. . . ." When the door at the bottom of the stairs had banged shut, Emma hurled the apple that she had been holding at the sloping roof above where the curly blond head had disappeared. Had Caroline still been on the stairs she would have been showered with smashed fragments and sap.

Emma stood for a moment clenching her hands, her whole body shaking. She bit her knuckles and then rushed into her own room and closed the door.

What she had considered her momentous revelation had barely touched the other girl's self-centered nature. Emma was furious at being so disregarded, so unconsidered, so denied. It was as though Caroline Heatherington had erased Emma's very existence and that of her family – and as though Emma had to exert every effort of personality and will to recreate them.

144

Deliberately she relaxed and unclasped her hands. She picked up the tinderbox that had been her father's and curved her hands gently around it. Holding it, she went to the quarter-pie window and looked out at the wooded rise of land where, only a few days ago, she had imagined walking with her mother. Gradually she stilled the turmoil inside her. Here, so high up, she always had the sense of being above and detached from the ground-level world of mud and work and subservience. From here she could look down on it but also gaze over the roofs to the hills beyond the town, now hidden by the falling rain. And here, now, she regained some of her self-control. Caroline Heatherington had not really erased her; the essential Emma could survive such careless and casual destructiveness.

She returned the tinderbox to the shelf and looked around the room that she was making her own, imprinting with her own personality. It was very neat and contained everything she possessed: her few clothes, the Bible she had inherited from Granny Wilbur, a single glove, and a copy of *The Colonial Advocate* that she had found on the street. There were also the book she had borrowed from Miss Morgan and the uncompleted shirt she was sewing for John.

After taking a deep breath and looking in the mirror to see whether the upheaval had messed her hair, she went to clean up the smashed apple and finish tucking the others in the sand. Then finally, exhausted and feeling as though she had been in the attic for a long time, she went downstairs.

At the foot of the attic stairs she met Miss Morgan just coming from her bedroom.

"The Major and Mrs. Heatherington are back, Emma."

"Yes, I'd heard. Have you spoken with them?"

"Oh, yes, and they've been very kind. They don't blame me in the slightest for their daughter's being out all night in that boat. Nor do they blame Mrs. McPhail."

"I'm glad. Indeed it was not your fault."

"No, but parents can sometimes be a little unreasonable where their daughters are concerned." She smiled but the signs of strain were still on her face. Emma realized that for two nights she must have had little or no sleep.

Miss Morgan started down the stairs to the lobby, then turned. "Oh, I almost forgot. Mrs. Heatherington would like tea in her room in about half an hour, after . . ." She nodded expressively toward the Heatheringtons' door, from beyond which the Major's voice sounded. "after they've talked to Caroline."

At the requested time, Emma took a tray up. Mrs. Heatherington was alone, unpacking her bag; when Emma came in she sat down with a tired sigh.

But she managed a smile for Emma. "I had a pleasant talk with your friends Mr. and Mrs. Wilbur," she said. "They sent you their love – and some apples." She handed Emma a cloth bundle containing perhaps half a dozen apples. "Mary wanted to send a kitten but I persuaded her not to."

"What on earth would I do with a kitten?" Emma said with a little laugh.

"What will you do with apples? There seems to be an abundance of them everywhere."

"They probably had nothing else to send," Emma said, her laughter gone as she remembered the Wilburs' meager life. "Are they all right?"

"They seemed to be. I was to thank you for the money and tell you that they missed you and John. They told me much about you, Emma, and all of it was good. They said you had looked after Granny devotedly and had been like one of the family."

"I did what I could. It was so good of them to take us in." Emma's voice failed as she remembered the fire, her last glimpse of her father with his clothes burning, and the summer-long strain of adjusting to life without her parents and with the kind but uninspiring Wilburs. She had to wrench her mind back to the present. "Did you like the farm?"

Mrs. Heatherington's face became serious. "We did, Emma. But we will have to reopen the discussion of the price with Mr. Blackwood. The farm is farther from Waterdown than he had led us to believe and the shanty, though well-built – we slept there one night – cannot with any justice be described as a cottage. Your friends Mr. Wilbur and Isaac Bates also felt that the asking price is too high. And now that we have seen it – that was your clever suggestion – we'll be in a better position to negotiate. We have a little time because we will not be able to buy it until we receive a legacy from England. The Major intends to seek further advice."

"That's a good idea."

"But we did like the farm, and the Major and I could live for a time in the shanty. He and Mr. Bates discussed turning the barn into a house, but I don't believe they reached any conclusion."

There was something dismissive in Mrs. Heatherington's voice; but Emma, before leaving, wanted to explain why she had carried the notes to the fort. Quickly she grasped at the first remark that occurred to her. "There has been . . . a certain amount of disturbance here while you were away," she ventured.

Mrs. Heatherington frowned. "We are very displeased with Caroline. My husband has gone to inquire about the two gentlemen who were involved in the fight."

"Perhaps I shouldn't have carried those messages, Mrs. Heatherington. But I hoped to be able to prevent the fight. I was too late."

"Even had you been earlier you might not have succeeded." She stood up. "Well, we'll hope that they both recover. I notice, by the way, that you've taken the bandage off your hand."

Emma held her hand out. "It's much better, you see."

Mrs. Heatherington examined the wound. "Yes, it's healing well."

"Thank you for looking after it – and for bringing the apples and the messages from the Wilburs."

At dinner that evening, Emma was surprised to see Mr. Jameson, the Dundas lawyer whom she had consulted a month earlier about her father's will and Mrs. McPhail's guardianship. He nodded a greeting and afterward, while she was clearing the table, spoke to her.

"I've come to York to attend my godson's wedding," he explained, looking as prosperous and complacent as ever. Emma remembered how much she had been in awe of him when she saw him in his office in Dundas; he seemed less formidable now. "I see you took my advice about going with your aunt rather than staying with your friends on the farm."

"Yes. But . . ." she said in a low voice and with a glance around at the remaining guests, "Mrs. McPhail seems to be unwilling that our family relationship should be known."

Mr. Jameson looked a bit startled; it was not clear whether this was a reaction to what Emma had said or whether he felt in some way reprimanded. "Oh! Well, no doubt it makes things easier. Are you enjoying York?"

Emma wondered about the former remark but answered only the latter. "I have not yet seen much of it. I work long hours here."

"It's a busy hotel," he said, neatly dodging her main point. "The work here will be excellent training for whatever you plan to do in the future." He nodded at her with enormous benevolence and then left her to her work.

From mealtime conversations during the next day or two, Emma learned that Captain Marshall was recovering from his wounds but that Captain Dixon's arm, which had been fractured in a complicated way, might not mend straight. Her own observations revealed that Caroline never left the hotel without the company of at least one of her parents.

But there was no news about the negotiations for the farm until the evening of the second day after the Heatheringtons' return. Emma and John were sitting in Emma's room in the attic. She tried to have a few minutes of private talk with him every evening before going to bed – though it couldn't always be managed – so that she could keep in touch with what he was doing and thinking. While talking, she usually kept busy with mending his clothes or sewing his new shirt but tonight her hands were too cold. John sat on the bed and Emma on the chair, each wrapped in a quilt, and she listened while John reported that the Heatheringtons had been at the livery stable that afternoon for a long talk with Blackwood.

"I don't suppose you heard what they said?"

"No, they were in the office – you know, the room with the window overlooking the yard."

"I wish we knew whether anything was decided."

"I don't think anything was."

"Oh?"

"When they came out, none of them looked very pleased and the Major said that he'd come again in a few days. That's what made me think that nothing was decided."

"You're probably right. And I suppose they haven't received their legacy from England yet."

John poked an arm out of the quilt to reach for one of the Wilburs' apples, which lay on the shelf above Emma's bed. Before taking the first bite, he asked, "They haven't said anything to you about the farm?"

"No, they haven't spoken to me since just after they came home."

He gave her a probing glance. "Well, I guess they're being careful on account of Mrs. McPhail. You still don't want her to find out that you talked." Then he bit into the apple.

The bald statement made Emma flinch, but it was a useful reminder that the need for secrecy remained.

John went on in his matter-of-fact way. "Have you been to see O'Brien, the man who knew Mother and Father?"

"I haven't had an afternoon free since Mrs. Delaney told me about him. I envy you sometimes, going into town with messages. But I'll try to talk to him tomorrow or Saturday afternoon. The apples are finished and so far I haven't been told about any other extra work."

"I'll come along if you like."

"To protect me?"

"No, silly, out of nosiness."

"Can you get time off in the afternoons for your own business?"

"I manage it sometimes," he said calmly. "Because of all those errands, no one asks if I'm not there. At least they haven't yet. So you could call for me. Just come in and look for me in the yard or the shed or the barn. I guess I'm allowed to talk to my sister for a minute. Then I can tell you whether I'm free to sneak out. But don't make it Saturday afternoon. The man at the Anchor won't have time to talk to you then. Saturday afternoons all the pubs in town are busy on account of the farmers coming to the market."

"I'll try tomorrow. But about this sneaking out . . . don't get into trouble, will you?"

He gave her a cool glance that made him look very grown-up, and even the grin that followed was that of an adult, wise and a bit cynical. She wondered whether it was a trick learned from the men or whether his mind and outlook were really as mature as they seemed.

THIRTEEN

Family History

When Emma went to call for John at the livery stable the next afternoon, she looked around with interest. She had never actually been in the yard before. It was a roomy area with Blackwood's house on the left and, to the right, an open drive shed sheltering three or four carriages. The stable was straight ahead. It was all quite well kept because Mr. Blackwood prided himself on catering to a better class of customer.

While she stood there, John appeared in the doorway of the stable. He saw her and, in the calmest way possible, stepped back inside and reached his coat down from a hook. As he crossed the yard he pulled it on and settled the lapels and collar. The sight of her young brother behaving in such an adult way gave a little tug at Emma's heart.

It took them only a few minutes to walk to the Anchor. They hardly spoke; Emma was not looking forward to this errand. However much she wanted information about her parents, she shrank from talking to the man who on that earlier occasion had looked at her with such strange and disturbing intentness.

But she had to go through with it, so when John held open the door of the tavern she composed herself to walk in calmly and with dignity. The half-dozen men in the room stared briefly at her, but Emma walked straight to the bar and addressed the man behind it.

"Are you Mr. O'Brien?"

"Yeah, what can I do for you?" His eyes shifted from Emma to John and then settled on Emma.

She had rehearsed her words carefully. "My name is Emma Anderson and this is my brother John. Mrs. Louise Delaney says that you knew our parents, and we've come to ask you to tell us what you can about them."

Again Emma felt at a disadvantage because of her ignorance. How galling it was to have to ask a stranger for information about her own parents!

She was watching O'Brien's face. Slowly the indifference that had been there at first dissolved into attention and curiosity and then into amusement. But it was an unpleasant, unfriendly amusement. Perhaps it was just that his broad, pock-marked face with the low forehead made his expression seem malicious, but all the same Emma shivered slightly.

He drew himself a tankard of beer, never taking his eyes off Emma's face, and settled himself comfortably against the counter.

"Well, now. Annie Taylor." He spoke with a drawl, as though he had all the time in the world, but his face was taut and his eyes were still full of that unpleasant sort of fun. "I remember her well. You look a bit like her. She'n her mother worked here, you know."

"Worked *here*?" Emma stared around her in sudden dismay. She had not expected that. The mother she had known was a ladylike person, though vigorous and hardworking. She had taught Emma courtesy, kindness, and, so far as frontier life permitted, a civilized and orderly housekeeping. But even as Emma tried to master her surprise and shock she realized that her parents had never spoken much about their earlier lives.

O'Brien laughed. "Didn't expect that, eh? Yeah, they worked in the Anchor. They come from somewhere east of here. Widow woman and a girl of . . . I don't know, mebbe about your age. Took a room here when they arrived – town was full 'n' this was the best they could do. Not what they was used to, though they was only farmers back home – gennelmen farmers, mebbe. My brother ran the place then. I was in the army – with a feller called Martin Anderson."

"That would be Father," Emma said unnecessarily.

"Martin Anderson," said O'Brien, dragging out the syllables. "Didn't know him well – he sort of kept with the gentry but we knew each other to speak to. Anyway, Annie Taylor and her ma come here looking for work – the big city, you know." He laughed harshly and drank again. "They thought they was gentry but all the same they needed work. They'd lived on a farm until old Taylor died and the womenfolk had to sell up to pay the debts. Naturally they was looking for *genteel* work."

Emma was hurt by the sarcasm but said nothing.

"Well, they didn't find none, and they hadn't much money, so before long my brother took 'em on to do the cooking and cleaning. Pretty soon Miz Taylor, the old lady, got sick – don't know what ailed her but she was poorly for a year or two until she died. She could still do some sewing and work like that, but Annie did the rest. After the old lady died, Annie stayed on. Useful wench she was."

He was obviously taking a wicked pleasure in telling the story. With the last words, however, his face darkened and his eyes left Emma's to dwell broodingly on his beer.

A customer called for service and O'Brien went to wait on him. As he did so, John gently nudged Emma and, when she looked down at him, tipped his head toward another figure behind the bar, a dim shape visible through the doorway at one end. It seemed to be that of an old man, and the face was touched by enough light to show that he was listening to the bartender's story. When O'Brien turned to put the customer's payment in a drawer, he saw the old man and, with a shooing noise and gesture, chased him away. But a moment later Emma saw him creep back.

"My brother," said O'Brien in explanation. "A soaker *and* a loony, if you can believe it. He lives here, out at the back, but I don't want him around the customers – he ain't good for business. Now, where was I?"

John spoke. "Is that the brother who ran this place when Mother worked here?"

"He's the only one I got."

"Did Father meet Mother here?" Emma asked.

"Don't know but I guess he must've done. Your pa was hurt at Queenston Heights and come back to York to get better. Stayed with his family, I guess."

"That would be his father and stepmother and Mrs. McPhail – who was a young girl then, Harriet Anderson," said Emma mainly to herself.

"Don't suppose he had any other family, did he? Well, when he got better he come here to see me – I was working with my brother – and I guess he met Annie. The old lady was dead by then." O'Brien stopped talking and stared somberly ahead of him. Then abruptly he drained his tankard and set it down with a crash that made a startled silence among the drinkers. The brooding look vanished and his eyes filled again with sardonic amusement. "In the end," he said very deliberately, "he married her."

Emma wondered what he meant by "in the end." Clearly a part of the story had been omitted – and O'Brien had left it out on purpose. If she asked about it, he would just laugh at her.

While she was thinking, John pushed something into her hand. It was a coin. Not until then had she realized that O'Brien would expect some payment in return for his information. Indeed, she should probably have offered to pay for his beer and have ordered something for herself and John. She was embarrassed to have overlooked it but, after all those years of living without any exchange of money, she still had to learn city ways. She laid the coin on the bar and slid it toward O'Brien.

"Thank you, Mr. O'Brien. We're much obliged to you."

He pocketed the money and sketched a military salute. "Pleasure. Glad I could . . . give you something to think about." He made a snorting noise that could have been a chuckle.

As she was turning away, something occurred to Emma. "Harriet Anderson . . . did you ever see her in those days?"

"Oh, sure, round and about. She was no more'n a girl, but quite the little lady. Her mother dressed her real good and sent her to school – some dame school here in town." He spoke indifferently now, neither brooding nor amused, and didn't wait for their good-byes before turning to serve another customer.

Emma and John walked back slowly. "What an unpleasant man!" she said at last.

"He's got a bad reputation."

"Did you notice that he left something out, some part of the story?"

"Yes. I wonder what it could have been."

"I'm sorry for Mother, having to work in such a place."

"The work must've been like what you're doing," John said with a quick glance at her, "but you're luckier than she was."

Emma had not noticed the parallel but now she thought about it. Indeed her position and working conditions were better than her mother's. How horrible it must have been for her! True enough, she had had the company of her mother in the beginning but later, when Mrs. Taylor became ill, she'd have been an addition to her daughter's work and worry.

Emma tried to imagine her mother working in the barroom where they had talked to Jack O'Brien. "Do you suppose she had to serve behind the bar?" she asked John. The place had been quiet on the two occasions when she had been there, but it must be busy sometimes. "I should have asked."

"I expect she did."

"And she never spoke to us about any of this. It must have been a very bad experience."

They walked in silence for a few minutes, then John laughed. "Trust young Harriet to be ladylike and get an education while Mother was a barmaid and slavey in a pub."

"Mother was a lady no matter what she did."

"But Mrs. McPhail hasn't done badly."

Emma would have liked to say something about the grimness of life and fate, the impossibility of understanding why her parents, after such a hard youth, should also have had to die such premature and horrible deaths. But though the angry, baffled feeling was strong in her, she couldn't shape the idea and find the words.

After dinner that evening, Mrs. McPhail said to Emma, "When you have finished clearing the table, will you please come to my room?" It was spoken quietly – a few of the guests were still about – but Emma heard something in her aunt's voice that made her hands and knees tremble.

"Yes, Mrs. McPhail," she answered, and stared with dread at the heavy tray that she had to lift with those shaking hands. By fussing with the salt cellar and some napkins she managed to keep busy until Mrs. McPhail left the room before taking up the tray and going out to the kitchen.

Ten minutes later she tapped at her aunt's door and was bidden to come in. Mrs. McPhail was sitting at the desk and gestured Emma to a chair beside it.

"I understand that you have been making friends with Major and Mrs. Heatherington."

Emma froze inside. It was a feeling she recognized from other occasions when Mrs. McPhail had found something out, and it immediately turned into a defensive wariness, an unspoken warning to herself to be very careful of what she said and of what her face might reveal.

"They have been kind to me."

"And clearly you have been kind to them." Though not loud, Mrs. McPhail's voice lashed out like a whip. Her hands twisted together in a knuckly knot and then hid themselves under the desk.

"Is there a law against kindness?"

"If there were I would hardly have taken you into my care, would I?"

"That was obligation – because of Father's will – and profit."

The last word lay between them like a dropped weapon. For a moment there was silence. A movement of Mrs. McPhail's elbows suggested that her hands were twisting again. Her face remained smooth, though something moved behind her eyes.

"How did you learn that the Heatheringtons were thinking of buying the farm that belonged to your late father?"

Emma shrugged. "I heard people talking."

"So you decided to put a spoke in Mr. Blackwood's wheel."

Emma did not deny it. Silent and less agitated now, she looked at her aunt, at the rather handsome face that not even anger could distort and at the cold gray eyes.

"And mine," said Mrs. McPhail.

This was the first time Emma had heard her aunt actually acknowledge that there was a business connection between herself and Blackwood. When Mrs. McPhail had introduced him to the Wilburs, on the occasion of his coming to inspect the farm, she had called him an acquaintance. But many little things had suggested a secret or unofficial partnership. And the conversation that Emma had overheard a few days ago had confirmed it.

But Emma was not going to pursue that matter now. She spoke deliberately and carefully.

"I did not like to see the Heatheringtons being fooled. Mr. Blackwood had not described the farm accurately to them."

"So you took it upon yourself . . ."

"I suggested that, as the weather was good, they might go and see it for themselves."

"It had not occurred to them to do that."

"They thought the distance too great and the season too far advanced. I suppose they are not familiar with Indian summer."

Put like that, it seemed a small and reasonable thing. But Mrs. McPhail was not finished.

"And what about your loyalty?"

"To whom, ma'am?" Emma asked with an ingenuous air that belied the hours she had spent fretting over this very question.

"To me, of course, as your guardian and employer."

"I didn't think it was right of you to . . . to cheat your guests. And John and me too."

There was a flicker in Mrs. McPhail's eyes; Emma wondered fearfully whether she had really gone too far now. Mrs. McPhail had admitted having a business connection with Mr. Blackwood – but could she possibly have been ignorant of his dishonest practices? Emma again remembered the conversation between them that she had overheard on Sunday afternoon and decided that she could not.

Mrs. McPhail's mind was apparently taking a different direction. "Cheat you and John?" she asked in a chilly voice.

"Well, I don't suppose you meant to divide with us your portion of the proceeds of this second sale."

"And if I did?" asked Mrs. McPhail with a change of expression, perhaps thinking that what Emma really wanted was a share of the profit for herself and John.

"I would still have wanted the Heatheringtons to be treated fairly."

They sat in silence for a moment.

"Since I learned about this, I have been wondering how to punish you," Mrs. McPhail resumed. Her voice was measured now; if she was still angry, she hid it. But Emma distrusted that appearance of calmness, and the reference to punishment made her tense. She was so completely at the mercy of this woman! True enough, the Heatheringtons had said that they would stand by her, but somehow Emma felt that the punishment would be something subtle, something about which it would be hard to complain. While waiting for the judgment, she kept her face as expressionless as possible.

Mrs. McPhail went on. "It seems to me now that the best procedure is for us to continue as we have been. I know you do not like your work, so it is a form of punishment in itself. Nor do you like me. The Heatheringtons will no doubt be leaving the hotel soon and their departure will deprive you of that support. Naturally I will be keeping a closer watch over you from now on. And if you run away like your predecessor in the job . . ." She shrugged. "I imagine that being a fugitive would be punishment of another sort. That will be all. Good night."

As soon as Emma was out of the room, her courage and control vanished. She began trembling so violently that she had to lean against the wall. Fortunately the lobby was empty.

But she could not stay here – Mrs. McPhail might come out at any moment. Leaning on the counter, Emma staggered to the front door and out onto the veranda, closing the door behind her. There in the cold, windy darkness she leaned against a pillar and gulped fresh air.

She had won, at least partially. It seemed that Mrs. McPhail and Mr. Blackwood would have to accept a smaller profit on the farm. And she herself had put her case to Mrs. McPhail and survived the response.

The lightness of the punishment struck Emma. Of course Mrs. McPhail had a position and image to maintain, but no outsider looked very closely into other people's way of disciplining servants. Rather it was as though the light penalty reflected Mrs. McPhail's awareness of the weakness of her own case. Had it been stronger, she might have dealt more harshly with Emma.

Then Emma's trembling turned into shivering. Unwilling to go in by the front door and risk meeting Mrs. McPhail again, she went round to the kitchen. There she found warmth and quiet, and Mrs. Jones just putting away her account books. Emma warmed herself for a few minutes and then, exhausted, took her candle and jug of water and went up to bed.

FOURTEEN

A Cottage

When the market-bound farmers woke her the next morning, Emma lay staring at the moving patterns of light that the torches and lanterns cast against her ceiling. How strange it had been yesterday to have two such momentous conversations in the same day! From the one with Jack O'Brien she had learned something about her mother; from the one with Mrs. McPhail she had learned something about . . . mostly about herself, probably, and about her aunt. Knowledge, information . . . several times she had felt helpless and vulnerable without certain kinds of knowledge, but she was not at all sure that what she had learned yesterday would make her stronger.

For the immediate future, obviously, that new knowledge would not change anything. The drudgery would continue.

Mrs. McPhail had after all devised a most effective punishment. And it was no consolation to Emma to know that her mother had formerly done the same kind of work but under much grimmer conditions.

For a moment she wondered whether she might not be able to find other work. But even if Mrs. McPhail let her go, what was she qualified for? Only for what she was doing now. And though there were probably better positions than this one, there were certainly worse ones as well.

She brooded over it while dressing and cleaning the downstairs rooms. By the time she was setting the table for breakfast, she was near tears and had to clench her teeth and blank her mind in order to keep going.

Mr. Jameson was the first of the guests to come down. He was in a good mood. While waiting for breakfast, he stood at a window looking out at the cold sunny day and stroking his waistcoat. After a few moments he turned to Emma, who was surveying the table to make sure that everything was set out properly.

"Well," he said, "It's a fine day for a wedding. A bit chilly, but dry. That's the main thing for a wedding, isn't it, to have dry weather?"

"Is your godson's wedding today, sir?"

"Yes, indeed. Important occasion for the boy."

"And for the girl, too."

"Of course, of course." He looked at her with an observant expression that she remembered from her interview with him in Dundas. Perhaps he had just remembered that she was also a girl.

Since his arrival at the hotel, Emma had hoped for a chance to have a private word with him. She felt that she should take the opportunity to ask him for some advice or guidance. But beyond an inarticulate plea for help she had no specific question to put to him.

Perhaps he sensed something of this, because he glanced at her again. For a moment, in the quiet room where only the snapping of the fire was heard, some word of question or help hung in the air between them. But it remained unspoken.

"When do you return to Dundas, Mr. Jameson?"

"On Tuesday. I have some further business to transact here, and a social event or two to attend. I hope the weather holds for my return trip."

"Will you travel by the stagecoach?"

"No, by boat. The last one of the season leaves York on Tuesday. The boats are much more comfortable than the coaches."

"I'm sure they are," Emma said, recalling her two days on the coach. "Excuse me, I must go and see about breakfast."

As she went to the kitchen, she regretted the unspoken word but realized that, with the rest of the guests likely to come in at any moment, there would have been little chance to talk. All the same, she would be sorry if, when he departed, they had talked about nothing but the weather.

As the morning progressed, Emma found her depression lifting. The bright day made her feel energetic and she resolved that, if she could go out in the afternoon, she would walk up Yonge Street, in the direction from which the farmers with their cattle had come that morning. So far all her walks had been south, into town.

But nothing came of it. Immediately after lunch, Mrs. McPhail appeared in the kitchen and said she would like all the staff except Mrs. Delaney to gather there. Joseph Tubb, whom Emma had been sent to fetch, grumbled something about "Old Harriet," and young Joe was not to be found. Mrs. Tubb was still washing the last of the lunch dishes and was told to continue; with the scullery door open, she could hear everything well enough. So it was Mrs. Jones, Joseph Tubb, and Emma who joined Mrs. McPhail at the long table.

Mrs. McPhail explained first about the committee for the relief of needy immigrants, of which she was a member. "Many of the immigrants require help for only a few days before they travel on to the backwoods settlements. They lack money, or are unwilling to spend the little they have on lodgings here in town, so they need temporary help until they acquire land of their own or find work.

"The other kind is more troublesome. They come here without definite plans but expect to find a land of plenty, where a livelihood is simply waiting to be picked up. These people quickly become a burden because they either rely on charity or turn to crime. Our committee helps them to find honest employment – and, of course, shelter.

"We, the members, realize that we must set an example for the rest of the town, so I have said that I can give short-term accommodation to some of these people."

Mrs. McPhail paused but no one said anything; the servants were waiting to find out how all this concerned them. Emma had a moment's alarmed vision of strangers sleeping in rows across the attic. Then Mrs. McPhail resumed.

"I intend to put at the disposal of the immigrant committee a small house that I own. It is located on Berkeley Street."

Emma hid her surprise. The faces of the others were also

unexpressive; presumably they were all used to having things sprung on them by Mrs. McPhail.

"I've agreed to have the house ready for occupation by Monday, so this afternoon Joseph and Mrs. Tubb and Emma will clean it. A cart from Mr. Blackwood's stable will be here shortly to take you and your cleaning equipment there. In the course of the afternoon, the cart will also deliver bed straw to fill the mattress covers, which are there already. It will deliver firewood – which is to be unloaded and piled neatly in the kitchen so that it is safely inside the house when you leave. Be sure to lock up carefully – we are not preparing the house for the use of thieves and vagrants."

After Mrs. McPhail left the kitchen, they filled several baskets with cleaning supplies and got themselves ready.

"Here, Emma, you take my shawl," Mrs. Jones said. "And tie it around yourself good and warm. There's nothing so chilly as an empty house, and you're only just getting over that cold."

Emma received the loan gratefully. "Do you think we could light a fire in the kitchen?" she asked, "It will use up some of the firewood, but . . ."

"It don't see why not. You'll freeze else. I put a jug of beer in one of them baskets and you can heat that if you want, for something hot to drink."

Once she was on the cart, Emma began to enjoy herself. She occupied the seat beside the driver, Fred Baker. The Tubbs sat in the back, behind the firewood and cleaning supplies, with their legs dangling.

"You must be the Fred that my brother mentions," she said.

Fred, who had a scrubby beard and one eye that wandered in its socket, grinned at her in friendly fashion. "Young Johnny. Good lad." He clucked to the horse.

Emma was at a loss for further conversation but Fred wasn't. He remarked, "Trust Old Harriet to turn that house o'hers to use – and earn herself a name for being a do-gooder at the same time."

Emma had only to turn toward him with an inquiring look for him to continue.

"It belonged to Will Hubbard, her first husband. They lived there till he died – coupla years after they was married, I guess."

"Isn't it in the district where the air is bad? Did he die of that?" Emma was not exactly sure how bad air killed people, but everyone said it did.

"Who knows?" Fred gave a shrug that rippled down the reins and made the horse shake its head. "He was sick and then he died. Old Harriet went to Boston. That was before she had the hotel, o'course."

"Leaving the house empty?"

"Nope, I rented it, I got married about then."

"Weren't you worried about the bad air?"

He winked his wandering eye. "Not me! Lived in them parts for years and it never bothered me none. 'Sides, Old Harriet couldn't *ask* much rent and I couldn't *afford* much. Suited us fine, me'n my wife. We live next door now, in a bigger house we built ourselves, and when Old Harriet's place is empty I sort of keep an eye on it and m'wife uses the back garden – she's got a little business, selling vegetables door to door. O'course Old Harriet'd like to sell but I guess there's no takers."

The trip was not a long one.

"There she is," Fred said and turned the horse into an unfenced, overgrown front yard.

The house was a one-storey log cabin. Fred drove up to the door and, after clambering off the cart, opened the padlock with a key from his pocket.

Inside there was one fair-sized room with a fireplace and two small rooms, each containing a bedstead. The main room was furnished with a table and benches, a settle by the fire, and open shelves here and there against the walls.

As Mrs. Jones had predicted, it was piercingly cold. Emma laid some kindling ready while Fred went to his house next door to get a shovelful of burning coals. Then he fetched water from his well, and a bucket of hot water contributed by his wife – "to dilute that there liquid ice." That done, and the cart having been unloaded in the meantime by the Tubbs, he drove off.

The three left behind worked in almost complete silence. Whether the Tubbs would have talked to each other if she had not been there, Emma didn't know. As it was, the only exchanges were requests for more water from the well or assistance in moving the furniture. Of his own accord Joseph went to wash the outsides of the windows. Emma, doing the insides at the same time, could see that the water he used began to freeze even as he worked, making lacy patterns around the edges of the panes. It was a cold day for late October.

Joseph also inspected the privy and, finding the door hinges stiff, borrowed a bit of grease from Fred's wife. When Fred came back with the cart, he and Joseph unloaded the few basic cooking utensils and the bedding that Mrs. McPhail had sent for the immigrants' use and helped Emma stuff the mattress covers with bed straw.

After the work was finished, all four of them sat for a few minutes by the nearly dead fire and drank the beer supplied by Mrs. Jones. Fred warmed his by stirring it with the fire-heated poker. Then they loaded the cleaning supplies onto the cart and locked the door carefully behind them.

As Fred drove away, Emma turned to look back at the little house. She felt oddly attached to it, in spite of its belonging to Mrs. McPhail, perhaps because she had cleaned it, or perhaps because she had tended the fire and sat beside it with her three odd companions, or perhaps because it was a pleasant little place. If it weren't for the bad air, a person could live there quite comfortably.

The next day was Sunday. After church, to take advantage of what remained of their free afternoon, Emma and John walked down to the lake and then toward the fort. This was the stretch of Front Street that, so far, Emma had seen only by night. Now, in the daylight, she admired the handsome, self-confident houses with their well-kept gardens.

They went as far as the tavern near the gates of the fort. "I can't read the sign," Emma said as they approached, squinting at the board that swung in the wind. "What's it called?"

"'The Greenland Fishery,'" John said. "Don't ask me why. It's very popular with the soldiers."

On their way back, he named the owners of some of the houses, clearly proud to be able to show off his familiarity with the town. "Mr. Blackwood hires out horses and carriages to them sometimes, and I have to take messages."

"Does he ever send you out alone with a horse?"

"Not yet. He says the horses are too high-spirited and not used to me. But come spring I'm to start leading them, and then after a while I can be hired out with a carriage. I'm to have a good suit of clothes then, and a hat and cape."

"That's wonderful," she said with a touch of envy, seeing no prospect of a comparable improvement in her own position.

It was along Front Street that they encountered Mr. Jameson emerging on foot from the gate of one of the big houses. Emma was not at all sure that he would deign to notice her but he did. He even walked with them. Remembering that he had not met John, she made the introductions. "John works in Mr. Blackwood's livery stable," she said.

"Ah, yes. I've met Mr. Blackwood. How do you like working in the stable, young man?"

"Very much, sir. I like horses."

"Then it seems you're well suited, as Emma is in your aunt's hotel."

Emma wanted to protest that she was not well suited but was aware that Mr. Jameson did not wish to hear such things. By glances or other reactions he showed that he noticed and perhaps even registered them, but he would never discuss them. This habit annoyed Emma, but there was nothing she could do about it. That was how he was.

Instead of protesting, therefore, she found another subject of conversation. "A few days ago John and I met an old friend of Father's, a Mr. O'Brien, who was in the army with Father but is now running a tavern. He told us something about Mother too."

"Ah, you're interested in your forebears. I'm sure there are other people besides this . . . this publican who knew him, though of course there has been much coming and going of people in York since then."

"I don't know of anyone else. Mrs. McPhail, when I asked her, was not helpful." Emma kept her voice noncommittal but she looked at Mr. Jameson and caught his quick, observant glance.

"I wish I could help you – I mean in finding friends of your parents'. But I didn't know your father at all; I saw him only on the occasion when he made his will."

"He didn't speak of anyone then?"

"If he did, I have forgotten. It was years ago, and I make many wills for people like him."

"It's hard to imagine him and Mrs. McPhail being related to each other. They are so very unlike."

"That can sometimes happen with brothers and sisters, especially if they take after different sides of the family." And he talked about families he had known.

When they turned up Yonge Street, Emma made a decision. If she were to get any help or information from him, it would have to be now. She could not talk freely in the hotel, and in any case he was leaving on Tuesday. She waited for the end of a sentence and then said, "Mrs. McPhail and I do not agree very well, Mr. Jameson. Am I compelled to work for her until my twenty-first birthday, when she stops being my guardian?"

"You are not compelled by law to work for her at all. She is only, as you say, your guardian. But in another capacity she is now your employer. If your parents were alive, you would work for them on the farm. You wouldn't think of them as employers but that is what, in a sense, they would be."

"But if I were to find other work?"

"Then you would have to handle the matter as any employee would: give notice of when you intended to leave. Even though you went to work for someone else – and perhaps even live elsewhere – you would remain Mrs. McPhail's ward. But your position in the hotel is not necessarily tied to your position as her ward. You are not her slave – she is your guardian, not your owner."

Emma thought that over.

"Have you another position in mind?" he asked.

"Not just at this moment, but I don't like the prospect of being a chambermaid forever."

"What would you rather do?"

"I don't know – something more responsible, more interesting, something that is not *all* hard physical work."

"No doubt you will marry in a few years."

"How can that be? I meet hardly anyone except the hotel guests, and they wouldn't marry a chambermaid."

He gave a jovial laugh that grated on Emma. "Stranger things have happened! But I am pleased that John is happy in his work."

John, who had been listening carefully, said, "I don't work for Mrs. McPhail, though."

Mr. Jameson continued talking to Emma. "Your present work gives you useful experience."

"Useful for what, sir? Only for more chambermaiding."

Mr. Jameson was silent. Emma had wondered whether it would be possible to involve him, to start him thinking about her situation. She was not sure whether she had succeeded.

"Would you like me to speak to your aunt?" he asked at last.

For an instant Emma's spirits lifted. She *had* involved him, and he had offered to help! Then immediately they dropped again. Mr. Jameson could have nothing particular to propose to Mrs. McPhail, and anything less than a definite plan would only look like interference, revealing that Emma had been complaining to outsiders. That would infuriate Mrs. McPhail and worsen Emma's position.

Besides, Emma dimly felt that it was too late now for anyone to help her in this way. For more than half a year she had been speaking and planning and deciding for herself; no one could do it for her anymore. She could not step back into childhood.

That bleak recognition kept her silent for a bit longer. But they were approaching the hotel and Mr. Jameson had not yet had his answer. This time it was her turn to be smooth and reserved.

"Thank you, Mr. Jameson, but no. I think my best chance is to look about me for other work."

"If I hear of anything, I will mention your name and let you know."

So they parted on cordial terms. Emma had learned two valuable things in the course of that conversation, two things that both related to her independence, one a sort of blessing and one a sort of doom.

FIFTEEN

Betrothal and Change

A rainy Monday morning – and the first of November," Miss Morgan said when she came downstairs for breakfast the next day. "Tea, please, Mrs. McPhail." She took her usual chair and reached for the toast and the currant jelly.

Mrs. McPhail handed the cup of tea to Emma, who was standing beside her. "For Miss Morgan, Emma. And would you attend to the fire, please? It doesn't seem to be burning very well."

"Yes, Mrs. McPhail."

Kneeling in front of the fire, Emma heard Miss Morgan mention finding a house that might be suitable for her school.

"Have you any idea yet of the number of pupils you might expect?" Mrs. McPhail asked.

"People are very reluctant to commit themselves. They assure me that I have only to open my doors and the girls will come flocking. I'd prefer something more definite."

Caroline Heatherington came down next. She drank hot chocolate and played with a slice of toast. In a minute her mother joined her.

"Has Caroline told you her good news?" she asked of the company in general. "She is to be married to Captain Dixon at the end of this month."

Caroline looked up for a moment, her face set and expressionless, and then down again.

Miss Morgan said the right things, and Caroline gave a little bow in acknowledgement.

"How is Captain Dixon now?" Miss Morgan went on. "He must be recovering from his injury if he is planning matrimony."

Mrs. Heatherington answered. "He is recuperating reasonably well, although his arm is still in splints. It may never be quite strong again and he is therefore applying to be transferred to the Lieutenant-Governor's guard of honor. Sir John Colborne values Captain Dixon highly."

"That bodes well for your future, Miss Heatherington," said Miss Morgan.

"Yes, I suppose it does. I shall prefer that to having him in the regular service."

They went on to discuss the availability of houses for the young couple and gradually Caroline's spirits seemed to lift a bit, though Mrs. Heatherington continued to watch her unobtrusively. Emma, going back and forth between the kitchen and parlor, puzzled over the girl's mood. Perhaps Caroline was reluctant to marry Captain Dixon or was not yet used to the idea. Perhaps she longed for Captain Marshall still. It could hardly be that she would have preferred to go to the farm with her parents.

That afternoon, as Emma was passing through the lobby, she was beckoned to the window by Mrs. Delaney. "Come and see, Emma!"

"What is it?" Emma asked, going to the window.

Out on the street, drawn up at the door of the hotel, was a carriage. It was a splendid shiny affair – shiny between the mud splashes, at least – and had a colorful coat of arms on the door. Four handsome chestnut horses shook their heads and switched their tails. A coachman sat on the box and two footmen stood nearby, apparently unaware of the rain and mud.

"Lady Colborne's carriage," whispered Mrs. Delaney.

"Why is it here?"

"Come to fetch Miss Heatherington to tea at Government House."

"Goodness!"

Just then Caroline came down the stairs looking a good deal happier than she had done that morning. She was wearing a short fur cape over a dress of rose-colored velvet. With a friendliness that was not typical of her, she gave a little wave of the hand to Emma and Mrs. Delaney as she passed through the lobby. One of the footmen assisted her into the carriage. Both footmen jumped on behind and the whole equipage moved off, its dignity only slightly marred by the dirty road and jolting progress. Emma, continuing her interrupted work, felt a little glow from having seen such a sight. Until recently, she had never really believed that the references in books to footmen and coaches with crests on their doors were anything but the authors' inventions.

The carriage had hardly disappeared when Major and Mrs. Heatherington ordered a fire to be lit in their room and tea to be brought. When Emma arrived with the tray, she found them sitting at the table amid a welter of papers.

"Oh, dear," said Mrs. Heatherington in an unusually agitated way. "There's nowhere for Emma to put the tray." She began shoving the papers together to clear a space on the table but her husband stopped her.

"We've just sorted these papers, Jane. The tea tray can go somewhere else – on the little round table, perhaps, Emma."

As Emma turned away to put the tray down, Mrs. Heatherington made a sound that might have been a suppressed sob and then blew her nose. Emma kept her back turned as she laid the fire and lit it with the burning candle brought along from the kitchen for that purpose.

"Will that be all, Mrs. Heatherington?" she asked, wondering if that sound had been a sob and, if so, what had caused the lady's distress. She wished that she could hug her as she would have hugged her own mother. "Shall I pour your tea?"

"No, thank you, Emma. I'll see to it. That's all for now." She looked up but did not quite meet Emma's eyes.

Major Heatherington was frowning over a column of figures. The room seemed to be full of their uneasiness or unhappiness. Emma wondered if after all they did not like their daughter's marriage or if they were in financial trouble or if perhaps they regretted having come to Upper Canada. As she left the room and shut the door quietly, she felt a sudden burst of angry helplessness at all the wrong and sad things in the world that could not be remedied.

When she returned to the kitchen, she found Mrs. Jones

standing with arms akimbo at the back door. She was glaring at a woman who stood in the yard with a lanky man and two children clustered around her. At their feet lay two small wooden chests and some cloth bundles.

"We was sent here for the key," the woman said doggedly. The one sad knot of ribbon on her bonnet trembled.

"This is a respectable hotel. The man at the wharf should not have sent you here." Mrs. Jones' whole body expressed indignation and contempt.

"Respectable! We're as respectable as . . ."

The man stepped forward, laying one hand on his wife's shoulder and taking off his hat with the other. "Scuse me, mistress," he said deferentially to Mrs. Jones, "but it's too late to tell us *not* to come here because . . . we're here, you see. All we want is the key and then we'll be on our way."

"Shall I fetch Mrs. McPhail?" Emma asked Mrs. Jones.

"Yes, please," said the cook, turning away from the new-comers with a toss of her head. "Be so good as to tell her that the immigrants are *at the door*."

Emma found her aunt behind the counter in the lobby, looking up something in the register of guests. "The immi-grant family have come, Mrs. McPhail. They're at the back door asking for the key to the house on Berkeley Street."

"They should have been sent directly to the house and told to ask Mrs. Baker for the key."

"So Mrs. Jones has been telling them. She seems . . . rather annoyed."

Emma's eyes and Mrs. McPhail's met. For the very first time an almost friendly look, faintly amused in the mutual recogni-tion of what lay behind Emma's words, flickered between them. Emma was so surprised at this moment's rapport that she simply stared as her aunt closed the register and came around the end of the counter. "I must pacify Mrs. Jones, then," said Mrs. McPhail as she walked swiftly to the kitchen.

By the time Emma had gathered her wits and returned to the scene, Mrs. McPhail was in the yard taking the newcomers' names. "Mrs. Ellen Berry, Mr. Stephen Berry, Young William, and Dotty."

"Bill," said the boy.

"Bill Berry," Mrs. McPhail amended calmly. She turned to the woman. "Where have you come from?"

"Burford," said Mrs. Berry curtly.

"And where is Burford?" Mrs. McPhail asked. "I don't believe it's a well-known town, is it?"

The man again came forward. Emma wondered if he spent his whole life smoothing over the effects of his wife's manners and temper. "That's near Oxford, ma'am. In England. And . . ." He glanced at his wife who was looking around her with an assessing air as though contemplating buying the hotel. "And I'd like to say that we're real grateful for . . . for the loan of this cottage of yours."

"It's only until you find work or take up some land. They did make that clear to you, I hope."

That reached Mrs. Berry. "Don't you worry none, ma'am. We didn't come all this way just to live on charity. We're going to do a lot better'n that."

"I'm very glad to hear it," Mrs. McPhail replied in a rather chilly voice.

But they couldn't stand in the yard all afternoon. Mrs. McPhail decided that the immigrants should have enough food for their first meal. She went into the kitchen to speak to Mrs. Jones – Emma had never heard her sound so conciliating, even to guests – and a basket was packed with a loaf of bread, a piece of cheese, some leftover ham, four small pastries, and a good-sized bottle of beer.

"Where's Joe?" asked Mrs. McPhail. "He can carry this and show the way to the house on Berkeley Street."

But Joe was not to be found, and Joseph was away doing an errand for one of the guests, so Emma had to go. She was given the basket and told to get the key from Fred's wife, Mrs. Baker. Out in the yard, the members of the Berry family picked up their bundles with an air of habit that indicated that each person had, long ago, at the beginning of the journey, been assigned his share and had taken it up and carried it untold numbers of times.

Mr. Berry, with one of the wooden boxes on his shoulder and the other carried by the rope handle, came to walk beside Emma. Mrs. Berry joined the children who, though subdued, seemed to be enjoying their new surroundings.

Emma asked the father about the trip from England. "I've never traveled, except just to come from the farm to here, and I can't imagine being on a ship, out of sight of land for all those weeks."

He was silent for a moment, as though searching for words. "It's long. You think it won't ever end, that the whole world's been turned to water. 'Nother flood, like in the Bible, and that tiny little ship looking like it ain't making any headway at all." He looked at her in an appealing way. "We lost our baby – she got sick and died. They . . . they put her overboard, into all that water."

"Oh, I'm so sorry. How old was she?"

"Just on two. You . . . you mustn't think badly of my wife. It hit her real hard and that always makes her cross. She . . .

she wanted to keep the dead baby and bury it when we got here, bury it where we could go to the grave sometimes. But the captain wouldn't let her – said he couldn't have corpses lying around. It hit her something awful. We left another one buried at home but my sister promised to visit the grave so that's not so bad."

He gave a deep sigh.

Emma tried to turn his thoughts in another direction. "Why did you come here?"

"Better prospects, we reckoned. For the young ones, too. We was tenant farmers at home and wouldn't ever have been anything else. I figure I'll have to work for someone else for a year or two, maybe, but after that I'll take up land and be my own man."

That was obviously a cheering thought. He shifted the box on his shoulder, walked more erectly, and looked about him as though challenging the world to keep him down any longer.

When they reached the little house, Emma was again charmed. She was half-sorry to think of the Berry family occupying it and half-pleased at its being lived in and not standing empty. She went next door and introduced herself to Fred's wife, a neat and bustling person with two small boys tumbling on the floor and a baby in a cradle.

"Here's the key, then, lass," she said, taking it down from a hook behind the back door. "It'll be nice to have neighbors there again. I'll tell them what they need to know. Wait a sec, I'll come along and meet them now. Mollie!" The whirring of a spinning wheel stopped and a girl of perhaps eleven came from another room. "I'm going next door. Watch the fire and the children, eh? Oh, and speaking of fire . . ." She scooped up some burning coals into a shovel. "They'll need this."

Emma took charge of the key and unlocked the door of the little house. Once inside, she unpacked the basket while Mr. Berry saw to the fire. Her leave-taking was barely noticed because all the others were busy making arrangements about water from the Bakers' well and milk from Mrs. Baker's cow.

In the next day or two Emma became sharply aware of the changeableness of hotel life. Since she had arrived, of course, guests had come and gone constantly, but those whom she considered her special people were longer-term residents.

Now, however, Mr. Jameson departed. It could not be said that he and Emma were friends, but she valued the acquaintance because he had made out her father's will and because he was a source of information and, sometimes, advice. When he left he tipped Emma fifteen cents and complimented Mrs. McPhail on her comfortable and well-run hostelry.

On the same day, at dinner, Miss Morgan told Mrs. McPhail about further plans she had made for her school. After Miss Morgan moved, Emma might see her occasionally about the streets but there would be far fewer contacts between them.

The Heatheringtons, too, would sooner or later buy property and leave the hotel.

Emma, reflecting as she cleaned the bedrooms, became depressed. She had formed ties with these people, had been interested in them, had shared their problems and pleasures. In return they had been kind to her. But she did not think it likely that these friendships would last when the people concerned were no longer living in the hotel. They would think of her, if at all, as the friendly chambermaid.

Suddenly she remembered, very clearly, what Mrs. McPhail had said on that first day in the hotel, when Emma had cleaned the room for the angry guest. Mrs. McPhail had warned her against speaking to the guests about personal matters. At the time Emma had been sure that her aunt was just trying to isolate her or keep the secret of their family relationship. But now she wondered whether Mrs. McPhail had been telling her – perhaps rather tactlessly – to avoid the kind of involvement that would lead to disappointment.

Who, then, was there for her to make friends with? Mrs. Jones was kind but was more a mother than a friend. Mrs. Delaney had something underhand in her manner that Emma distrusted. Mr. Blackwood? She disliked him thoroughly and he had been distinctly cool toward her recently, his joviality replaced by a sort of offended dignity. Emma wished she knew how much of his expected profit on the farm she'd caused him to lose.

None of them were available as friends. Would she ever meet anyone else? Drying the basin that she had just washed, she was baffled, depressed, and – though she hardly dared to admit it – frightened.

SIXTEEN

A Dinner Party

n the Wednesday afternoon of that week, Mrs.
McPhail called the whole staff together in the
kitchen. Mrs. Delaney was included – the door
between the kitchen and lobby was left open so that an eye
could be kept on the front of the hotel. Mr. and Mrs. Berry
were present too. Mrs. McPhail sat at the head of the long
table and Mrs. Jones at the foot.

"I've called you together," Mrs. McPhail began, "to plan a
very important event." She looked at each of them, her cool
gray eyes moving down one side of the table and up the
other. Emma wondered what all this portended.

"Today is Wednesday," Mrs. McPhail continued. "On
Sunday we will be giving the biggest and the finest dinner that
has ever been held in this hotel. Major and Mrs. Heatherington,

to celebrate their daughter's betrothal, are inviting a number of their friends, including Sir John and Lady Colborne, to dine here." For the benefit of the Berrys she added, "Sir John is the Lieutenant-Governor, the representative of His Majesty King William."

Mrs. Jones was counting on her fingers. "Only four days to prepare!" Her eyes widened as she stared at her employer. "It can't be done, ma'am. How many people altogether?"

"Fourteen."

"And all the regular meals in the meantime!" wailed the cook.

"It can be done and will be done, Mrs. Jones," said Mrs. McPhail calmly. "Mrs. Berry will assist you – and I want it clearly understood," she said as the two women glared at each other, "that Mrs. Jones is the mistress of this kitchen. That means that Mrs. Berry will have to take orders and Mrs. Jones will have to comport herself like a leader. After this general meeting, Mrs. Jones, you and I will go over the menu."

Mrs. Jones, grim with a sense of responsibility, nodded silently.

"Joseph, you and Joe and Mr. Berry will do the usual work of carrying wood and water and also help to rearrange furniture in the guests' parlor on the day of the dinner. On that day you'll also make sure that the path and veranda steps are swept and dry, and you will assist with the horses and carriages."

"Yes, ma'am."

"Mrs. Tubb will clean the parlor and lobby thoroughly and also one of the bedrooms, which will serve as a powder room for the ladies. Louise Delaney and Emma will wait on table, with Mrs. Berry carrying the food in from the kitchen. I will hire two extra servants for the occasion, a maid to attend the ladies in the powder room and a butler to serve the wine. They will be here only for that single day."

She paused and looked around the table again.

"Louise and Emma will have to be spotlessly clean and neat. Wear the best of your black dresses and I will provide ornamental aprons for the occasion. Pay special attention to your hair and fingernails, please."

Emma blushed at having such personal things mentioned before strangers, but she made a mental note all the same.

"Remember," Mrs. McPhail said, clasping her hands and leaning forward, "that if we manage this event well it will be a credit to us all, to the hotel and to you individually."

There was a murmur around the table as Mrs. McPhail rose.

"Mr. and Mrs. Berry will, of course, receive the usual wages and the rest of you may count on something extra at the end of the month. Now, Mrs. Jones, will you come with me to discuss the menu."

Nothing further happened that day except that Mrs. Jones went to the shops. But on the following morning Mrs. McPhail brought out a supply of fine damask tablecloths and napkins, crystal decanters and glasses, and silver. Washing, ironing, and polishing it was Emma's main occupation for the next couple of days.

She did much of it in the kitchen, where Mrs. Jones and Mrs. Berry were preparing food in awesome quantity and variety. "Twenty-five different dishes, to be served in three courses," said Mrs. Jones with satisfaction. "And more for the supper, o'course." When she saw that Emma was interested, she spent a moment now and then identifying snipes and a chine of pork, oysters and woodcock, explaining what a ragout was and a galantine. Already on Wednesday, after her expedition to the shops, a stream of delivery boys and carts came all evening bringing her purchases to the back door. On Saturday morning she went to the market and was followed home by Blackwood's cart laden with fish, meat, vegetables, and fruit. She and Mrs. Berry were up most of Saturday night and again early on Sunday morning.

Mrs. Jones was clearly pleased to have full scope for her abilities. Though she was occasionally irritable, everyone recognized that she knew her business and worked willingly for her, the men carrying endless supplies of wood and water, the boys tending the fires and taking out slops. Mrs. Berry turned out to have a light hand with pastry and was, besides, in a much better temper than she had been on her arrival. Mrs. Tubb housecleaned, waxed furniture, and polished brass.

Emma had been asked to wash her hair on Friday; hair-washing required hot water and Mrs. Jones declared that on Saturday there would be no room at either the kitchen or the wash-house fireplace for anything unrelated to cooking.

On Sunday morning the furniture in the guests' parlor was rearranged. The dining table was extended by placing two card tables against it, one at each end. Mrs. McPhail, supervising Mr. Berry and young Joe Tubb, explained her plan to Emma. "When dinner is over we'll move them away again for anyone who wants to play cards. Supper will be informal – people can sit at the dining table or the card tables, just as they wish. Or," she said with a gesture toward the arrangement of sofa and chairs at the other end of the room, "in what will have to pass for a drawing room."

Meanwhile, because the ground outside was muddy after a night of rain, Joseph and John were making a sort of portable wooden walk to reach from the veranda steps to the place where the carriages would stop.

Early on Sunday afternoon the two servants hired for the day arrived and, though supercilious in their manner toward the regular hotel staff, efficiently took charge of their departments.

Miss Morgan, the only guest in the hotel besides the Heatheringtons, obligingly went to spend the rest of the day with friends.

Mrs. McPhail spent some time directing Mrs. Delaney and Emma in the setting of the table with the damask, crystal, and silver. At the same time she gave them instructions as to what they were to do that evening. "Your main work will be to take away the serving dishes and plates at the end of each course and to bring on the next course. But be ready at all times to serve the guests whatever they ask for. I'll be carving at the dresser and you will hand around the platters of carved meat. The butler will attend to the wine."

A bit later, when Mrs. McPhail had inspected all the preparations minutely, and Emma had carried hot water up to the Heatheringtons' rooms, Emma herself went up to the attic to change. From now on she was not allowed in the kitchen so that her clean clothes would remain free of kitchen smells.

On coming down again, she noticed how quiet the front rooms of the hotel were. The lobby and parlor looked as though they were enjoying their own gracious dimensions and handsome appointments. The fire burned clear behind the gleaming brass firedogs. A generous number of candles had been lit so that a multitude of flames was reflected in the silver and crystal, and glowed in the ruby and gold depths of the decanters' contents. The waxed floors shone and the curtains, cleaned and pressed, hung in elegant long lines over the windows.

For probably the very first time, Emma was alone in the front rooms of the hotel with leisure to look around and notice things as objects in themselves rather than as things to be cleaned or moved. They gave her the feeling she had had once before of being made richer. Ever since she could remember, she had longed for beautiful things – not to own them, necessarily, but to nourish her spirit on them. In these last few days she had handled more beautiful objects than ever before in her life, and she did feel better for it. Besides, she now realized that the hotel building itself was handsome, dignified, and well proportioned. She knew nothing about architecture but had been comparing the hotel with other buildings in York, and she sensed the rightness of it.

Mrs. McPhail interrupted her reverie by bringing out the lace-trimmed aprons for Emma and Mrs. Delaney. Emma fingered the fabric with pleasure. Mrs. McPhail was wearing lace too – white lace collar, cuffs, and cap with her black dress, which, though like her everyday dresses in style, was made of finer fabric.

Then the Heatheringtons came down from their rooms, the Major in uniform with his ribbons on, Caroline in a soft blue gown trimmed with silver thread and white fur, and Mrs. Heatherington in maroon. Both gowns had enormous puffed sleeves, and both ladies wore feathery headdresses. For a few moments they and Mrs. McPhail stood talking in the lobby. Then Mrs. Heatherington went to look at the dining table.

"Nervous?" she asked Emma, who had followed her.

"Yes, I'm afraid so."

"There's no need to be. You will do very well, as always. Just remember that your task is to serve the guests and add to their enjoyment of the meal."

Emma was grateful. "I hope it goes smoothly," she said, managing a smile.

"I'm sure it will. Mrs. McPhail has organized everything beautifully."

Captain Dixon was the first to arrive. He and the Heatheringtons were to stand in the lobby to receive the other guests. His arm was in a sling and he looked very pale; the Major immediately took him to the parlor and persuaded him to drink some brandy. "To get you through this business, man."

Emma lost some of her anxiety as she realized that the Heatheringtons and Captain Dixon were nervous too. The four of them and the hotel staff, usually on opposite sides, were for this occasion united as hosts facing the ten guests still to come.

At the last moment, Mrs. McPhail stationed Emma on the first landing of the staircase so that she could direct the ladies to the powder room. This, as it turned out, gave her a perfect position from which to see the arrivals.

Two officers and their wives came first. The lobby was suddenly full of hearty voices, self-confident gestures, and a multitude of scents. In a few minutes the gentlemen went into the parlor and the ladies, talking together and moving slowly, came up the stairs toward which Mrs. McPhail had directed them. They seemed to need no help in finding their way and appeared not even to notice Emma. She observed them, however, carefully noting the velvet cloaks with embroidered collars, the low straight necklines of the gowns, the delicate shoes whose tips showed under the slightly lifted skirts.

When the two ladies had disappeared into the powder room, Emma's attention turned again to the lobby. Someone said, "The Colbornes!" and there was a rustle among the welcoming party.

Mrs. McPhail opened the door and stepped aside to admit the Lieutenant-Governor and his lady. Emma watched rapt as those in the lobby bowed and curtseyed. Then there were greetings and handshakes. Lady Colborne said something complimentary to Mrs. McPhail about the immigrant committee – the two of them had apparently met in connection with it – and Mrs. McPhail was introduced to Sir John Colborne. Though deferential, she spoke easily with these distinguished people – but then, Emma could not imagine her daunted by anyone.

Emma gazed delightedly at these special guests, the representatives of the King. There could be no doubt of their dignity and importance, yet they talked in informal and friendly fashion with the Heatheringtons, Captain Dixon, and Mrs. McPhail. Sir John laughed at something Dixon said, and Lady Colborne walked over to admire the grandfather clock.

Then Emma, realizing that Lady Colborne would come directly past her as the other ladies had done, froze in fright. She ought to curtsey – but it had never occurred to her to learn! The ladies in the lobby had curtseyed so quickly and gracefully that Emma had not been able to see exactly how it was done – and, in any case, at that moment she had been paying more attention to the Colbornes.

For a moment all her pleasure was overwhelmed by panic. But, as it turned out, the problem solved itself. Mrs.

Heatherington was escorting Lady Colborne to the powder room. When the two ladies reached the landing where Emma stood, there was no space left for Emma to perform even a small curtsey. So she simply bent her head and dipped at the knees. She looked up in time to catch two kindly smiles.

After a few minutes, the remaining guests arrived, one couple shortly after the other. The ladies came up the stairs one by one, and Emma directed them to the powder room.

Then Mrs. McPhail beckoned her to begin her work in the dining room. Some of the first-course dishes had to be set out on the table before the guests sat down.

A screen had been placed so as to conceal the kitchen door from the guests seated at the table. Behind it, beside the door, was a table on which Mrs. Berry put the dishes as she brought them in. From there they were taken by Emma and Mrs. Delaney either directly to the table or to the dresser where Mrs. McPhail carved the meat and laid it out on platters. The wine was ranged on the dresser too, at the other end of the long counter, and presided over by the butler.

In each of the three courses there were meat, fish, and poultry dishes. In the first course there was also soup and several vegetables. In the second and third were some dishes containing oysters, rabbit, or fruit.

After the flurry of starting the first course, everything moved slowly. The guests asked for food from other parts of the table to be handed to them. Emma and Mrs. Delaney stood by to do this, and the butler moved about with wine. Mrs. McPhail, even when she had her back to the table while carving, seemed able to keep her eye on everything.

The two periods of clearing away one course and bringing on the next were busy, and Emma noticed how careful she and the other servants had to be not to get in each other's way. Mrs. Berry's comings and goings gave glimpses of the kitchen where everything seemed to be in a state of controlled frenzy.

When Emma overcame her first nervousness, she began watching the guests as people and listening to them. In the increasing heat and noise, faces became red and voices loud. People talked with their mouths full and increasingly interrupted each other. One of the gentlemen emphasized his words by crashing his knife handle down on the table. But none of this interfered with the eating and drinking. Emma and Mrs. Delaney carried around platter after platter, dish after dish. The butler, who had opened quite a few wine bottles before the guests arrived – "to let it air," he said – opened more as the dinner progressed. Mrs. Delaney asked why he was doing it behind the screen.

"This wine won't have had time to air," he said. "Those chaps are in no state to notice the difference, but all the same I'd rather not be seen actually pulling a cork."

Indeed, the voices and faces suggested that the distinction between aired and unaired wine would not be observed. Everyone now seemed to be talking and eating at the same time. Arms reached for dishes or beckoned the butler. Mouths opened to take food in and let words out. The elaborate hairdo of one of the ladies was coming loose and sagging slightly to one side. Emma had read in one of her father's books about such a meal; the author had clearly not exaggerated.

Among all the talk, Emma could not follow any one conversation. But she heard political terms like "reform" and "tory." While leaning forward between two of the people to serve them, she heard a few sentences about a new literary magazine that one of them had received from England. Someone mentioned a singer who had recently performed at Government House. There was some discussion about a possible change in the troops stationed at the fort.

Toward the end of the meal Emma's eye fell on Mrs. Heatherington, who was for the moment not in conversation with the gentlemen sitting on either side of her. She held her wine glass in one hand and with the other absently slid a fork slightly this way and that. Her eyes were very grave as they watched her husband and daughter at the other end of the table, and in a flash Emma thought of the cost of this dinner. *They can't afford it!* she realized, and it was as though the words had been shouted from Mrs. Heatherington's mind to Emma's. What she and the Major had said about buying the farm clearly showed that their means were limited, and Emma remembered that they had been making anxious calculations earlier that week. And this was not the only expense involved in the wedding.

As though aware of the girl's concentrated gaze, Mrs. Heatherington briefly lifted her eyes to Emma's. Her lips smiled but not her eyes, and then she turned to watch the butler refilling her glass.

When at last the speeches had been made and the dinner was over, the guests left the table. The ladies went up to the powder room, and Major Heatherington led the gentlemen up to his and his wife's bedroom where a close-stool was available for their easement. During the guests' absence the servants quickly cleared the table and rearranged the furniture.

Tea and coffee would be served after that and whoever wished could play cards. At the end of the evening, Emma and Mrs. Delaney would bring out a cold supper.

In the kitchen, Mrs. McPhail spent a few minutes with Mrs. Jones, surveying the leftover food, deciding what could be served to the hotel guests in the coming days, and ordering that to be put in the larder. That still left a great deal.

"This is for your dinner," she said to the servants, gesturing at the kitchen table on which it was all set out. "Take an hour now to rest and eat before you finish the cleaning up. But Louise and Emma must remember that they will still be required to assist at the guests' supper. You two must remain neat. Try not to get too hot, and tidy yourselves before going into the parlor again."

She took up a tray containing her own dinner, which she would eat in her room. "Oh, yes, one more thing. You may drink the wine in the opened bottles, and there's beer. And a glass of whiskey for each person who wants it." In the doorway she turned. "You did well, all of you. Thank you."

While Mrs. Jones drew a large pitcher of beer from the keg in the larder, all the others helped to lay places around the kitchen table. Then, exhausted but exhilarated, they ate their dinner. Except for the absence of hovering servants, they made much the same picture as the company in the dining parlor had done, and Emma was sure that she enjoyed the food every bit as thoroughly as Lady Colborne.

SEVENTEEN

Writing Letters, Hearing Stories

A few days later, after dinner, Emma was summoned to the Heatheringtons' room. She found both the Major and his wife there, sitting near the fire and drinking madeira.

"We wanted to tell you, Emma," the Major began, "that we have decided to buy your late father's farm."

"Oh, I'm so glad!" But even as she spoke she sensed that the Heatheringtons themselves were not entirely happy. They were looking tired and strained, and Mrs. Heatherington's eyes were less lively than usual. "I hope you are pleased about it," she added hesitantly.

"We expect to be contented there," said Mrs. Heatherington. "We like the neighbors and the scenery, though we still wish it were nearer to York. But we have

spoken to a gentleman who farms in Thornhill – a friend of
Sir John Colborne's – and with his help have come to a better
understanding of what farming in Upper Canada involves."

That, thought Emma, could well account for their mood.

"We have also," said the Major, "arrived at a more reasonable price with Blackwood. We do, however, find it necessary to move to the farm this autumn, immediately after
our daughter's wedding – or rather, as soon after that as
there is enough snow on the ground to make it possible to
travel by sleigh."

Emma stared. She had never imagined them going to the
farm before spring. "But you will have no supplies," she
protested. "No food stored, or firewood, or hay for a horse."

"The forest will supply firewood – there is plenty of fallen
timber. Mr. Wilbur offered to sell us some dry firewood to
supplement the wet. He also has hay and potatoes and some
other things. The rest will, of course, have to be bought in
the shops. But even so it will be more economical than spending the winter here."

"Yes, I suppose so." Emma noticed that there was no more
talk of cottages and parties of friends coming to visit. She was
sorry that those visions were gone but it was probably better
for the Heatheringtons to lose their illusions before they
moved to the farm than after.

"Thank you for telling me," she said. "I do hope everything works out well."

"Did your parents find it easy to adjust to farm life?" Mrs.
Heatherington asked.

"Well, you see, they had no adjusting to do. As children
they lived on farms here in Upper Canada. They were used to
the conditions."

"Yes, they would be."

Emma searched for something comforting to say. "I'm sure you will find the Wilbur and Bates families helpful. They'll be glad to have the farm occupied rather than lying empty. And you'll be leaving your daughter well settled and provided for."

"Yes," said the Major, "we are happy about the match she made. Our dearest wish now is that she will have a happy future life. We are doing all we can to ensure this. After these rather disturbed years – when her mother and I were away from England – she deserves it." His thin brown face was anxious still and for a moment no one spoke. Then he looked at his wife and his eyes brightened. "You and I, Jane, are starting a new phase of life just as she is."

Mrs. Heatherington smiled back, then turned to Emma. "Our real reason for wanting to see you is that we have a little gift for you – a keepsake to remember us by and something that we hope will ensure that we stay in touch with you." She went to the table and brought back a quill, a few sheets of paper, and a small, square bottle of ink. These she set down on the round table near Emma. "We thought you might find these useful, and we hope that they'll encourage you to write to us."

"Oh, Mrs. Heatherington!" Emma put out a hand to touch the little ink bottle and to stroke the soft edges of the quill.

"The quill and paper are new, of course," Mrs. Heatherington said, "but the ink bottle is one that I've had for some years. It has to be kept upright – it leaks when tipped because the stopper is glass and not cork."

"I'll think of you every time I use it, Mrs. Heatherington," Emma said. With a smile, she added, "And I'll try to remember not to tip it."

Major Heatherington spoke. "We've come to feel that you are in some sense one of us now, and we don't want to lose contact."

"It's very, very kind of you," she said, glancing from one to the other. "I'd love to write you and maybe, sometime, to visit. But of course you'll be coming to town now and then, won't you?"

"No doubt we shall," said Mrs. Heatherington, "but we shall look forward to your letters between visits."

"Oh, I'll be delighted to write you." She rose and gathered up her new belongings. "Thank you *very* much indeed."

It seemed to her that the giving of the present had cheered the Heatheringtons a bit.

In her room, she placed the writing materials on the shelf near the tinderbox – the Heatheringtons' gift close to the memento of her parents. Soon those four people would be linked in another way, through the ownership of the farm.

That evening, Emma reflected on the whole conversation and particularly on what the Major had said about their beginning a new life. It was true – and it surprised her because until now she had always thought that grown-ups stayed where they were and never did anything new. And she found something disturbing in the fact that adults like the Heatheringtons could be as insecure and uncertain as young people when they began something strange. Apparently it was not sensible to think – as she now realized that she had been doing – that adulthood automatically brought a solution to all the upsets and anxieties of youth.

She got up to stand at the quarter-pie window. Outside was thick darkness except for a faint glow in a window here and there, and her reflection stared back at her. In the light of her candle, her face looked hollow-eyed and gray, grave and elderly. It looked portentous, not an individual human face but an abstract image. Somehow it fitted with Caroline's marriage, with the modified hopefulness of the Heatheringtons about the farm, with Emma's own prospects. The gaunt reflected face said that this was the way things were, that hope and pleasure never came unmixed, and that growing up meant learning that.

One evening that week John was late coming home. This happened from time to time, usually when one of the carriages used on that day had to be prepared for hiring out to a customer early on the following morning.

Emma, doing some sewing, waited for him in the kitchen. Since her last confrontation with Mrs. McPhail, she had been watching carefully for any sign that Blackwood was taking out on John his resentment at Emma's involvement in the negotiations about the farm. John had reported that Blackwood was no longer very friendly – "but I hardly see him so it doesn't matter. I guess he could get rid of me but he hasn't yet."

Mrs. Jones was also in the kitchen. She had done her daily accounts and was now sitting by the fire, knitting a black stocking. Mrs. Tubb was in the scullery, finishing the dish-washing.

The clock in the lobby had just struck nine when the back door opened partially and John put his head in. "Emma? Can you come here a minute? Bring a handkerchief or something and the lantern."

She lit the lantern and flipped her cloak around her. There was always a handkerchief in the pocket of her dress.

The night was dark and the wind carried some large, wet snowflakes. John led the way to the woodshed. Inside, sitting on the chopping block and leaning back against the piled wood, was the most revolting figure Emma had ever seen. He was dressed in rags, layer upon layer of them. His hands were dirty and one of them was badly scarred and lacking two fingers. His head was bare except for wisps of gray hair. His face was red and looked raw and shapeless, and he had not shaved for some time. The stale, sour smell of him reached her where she stood.

"This is old Mr. O'Brien," John said to Emma. "Luke O'Brien, brother of the man we talked to at the Anchor. I helped him once to get away from some pestering boys and took him home. Now I found him again and he's hurt his knee. Can you bandage it?" He glanced up at her. "I thought he might know something about Mother and Father, but first have a look at his knee."

Emma had stayed in the doorway of the woodshed, desperately clutching the rough post beside her. At first glance, the ruined creature sitting on the chopping block recalled her experience on Henrietta Street – not the mockery and insult but rather her terror and the underlying evil. After John's voice stopped, there was a long moment while she still clung to the doorpost, grappling with that sudden upsurge of revulsion and fear. Then John's words sank in – *might know something about Mother and Father*. She realized too how gently and kindly he had spoken of the old man. If John could speak like that, it must be all right.

Just the same, it took an effort of will to let go of the post and step forward. The old man hadn't moved, but when Emma knelt in front of him and looked up, she met his eyes. There was something human in them after all, something detached from the wretched body, and the Henrietta Street memory faded. Only then did she look at his knee.

Through a great tear in his breeches, she could see the wound. The kneecap was dark with mud and blood. She was not skilled at medicine but she had hurt her own knee last year and remembered what her mother had done.

"You stay here," she said to John as she got to her feet. "I have to get a few things."

Mrs. Jones was still in the kitchen.

"We've got someone in the woodshed who's hurt his knee," Emma told her. "Have you got any healing ointment and some cloth for a bandage? And may I use this pail for water to wash it?"

"There's rags in the bag in the cupboard and ointment on the shelf – the green jar." Mrs. Jones made some common medications herself. "Take the old pail, and you can use some warm water from this kettle here."

Emma got everything together and returned to the woodshed, repressing her shudder at the thought of touching the filthy old man and his injured knee and his skinny, hairy leg. But John's suggestion about getting information kept her going.

The man winced as she washed the knee, applied ointment, and bandaged it. But when she sat back on her heels and looked up, he gave a little nod and his ruin of a face twitched in what might have been meant for a grin. His hand made a gesture toward the bandage.

"Whitest thing . . . I've had on me in years." The voice was ragged, hoarse, and hard to understand but Emma welcomed it. It came again. "I . . . seen you in the pub."

"Yes, we were asking about Anne Taylor. Our name's Anderson; Anne Taylor was our mother."

"Annie . . . and Martin Anderson." Luke O'Brien coughed horribly and spat, careful not to hit the young people who were squatting on either side of his outstretched leg.

"Annie Taylor worked for you," John reminded him.

"Should've married our Jack."

Emma and John exchanged glances. "Your brother Jack? Was he engaged to Anne Taylor?" Emma asked.

The face twitched again. "Disagreed . . . he said yes, she said no . . . Jack . . . took advantage. Had his way with her." Luke O'Brien glanced from one to the other with a doubtful look, as though wondering whether he should have told them this.

Emma caught her breath and looked at John, whose face was expressionless.

The old man went on. "Anderson fought him. In our yard . . . the pub yard. Men betted on the fight." There was a sound that might have been a chuckle. "Good for business . . . near as good as a cockfight."

"Did they fight with weapons?" John asked.

The incomplete hand moved slightly where it lay on the old man's thigh. "Fists . . . boots. Scandal. Anderson took Annie away, out of town. End of story."

John and Emma again glanced at each other. John stood up. "Will you help me take him home?" he asked Emma. "Or I can ask Joe."

"I'll help," said Emma, though suppressing another shudder. This was something that she and John had to do together.

And so, one on each side, they supported him through the

streets. The snowflakes came thicker but melted on landing, and Emma was glad of the lantern in the deep darkness. To judge by the scarcity of lights, most people were in bed.

When they reached the Anchor, John steered the way up the alley. The yard behind the pub – presumably the same yard where Martin Anderson and Jack O'Brien had fought over Anne Taylor – was dark and muddy. Under John's direction they approached a lean-to against the back of the main building; when they entered, Emma saw that it was built against what must be the kitchen fireplace and was heated only by whatever heat came from that source. It was just a shed, uninsulated and even incapable of keeping out the wind. They eased the old man down on a makeshift bed, no more than boards laid across logs to raise the occupant slightly above the damp earth floor. The bedding was a litter of straw and sacks.

"I don't know if he undresses," John said quietly. "I didn't try last time. He's probably warmer with his clothes on."

Emma bent over Luke O'Brien trying to get into his blurry and wavering field of vision. "Will you be all right now? Keep that bandage on for a few days, and have someone look at it if it starts hurting more. All right?"

Only his eyes nodded. His face was an unreadable mask. Emma felt terribly sorry to be leaving him. But what could she and John possibly do?

"Come on," John said, swinging the lantern a little. "It's late. I'll come and see him tomorrow."

When they were out in the street again, walking home, John spoke. "Fred Baker told me about Luke. He ran a fairly decent public house when he was in charge – nothing fancy but better than it is now. He always drank a little more than he should have but kept a check on it. When his brother Jack joined him after the war with the Americans *he* wanted to take over – didn't want to be just an assistant or even a partner. So he pushed Luke on to drink more. Gradually Jack took over and . . . and sort of spread stories about Luke, said things to give him a bad name. *Now* Jack tells everyone what a noble fellow he himself is to give bed and board to his poor sot of a brother."

"What he told us . . . do you think it's the truth?"

"It could be. It fits, doesn't it? That's the part Jack skipped over and that made him look so angry."

"When he said 'scandal' do you suppose he meant the fight over Mother? Or . . . or what Jack O'Brien . . . did to her?"

John was silent a moment. "Probably the fight," he said at last. "I guess the . . . the other was private and secret. But the fight . . ." John's voice tightened. "I just hate the thought of people gathering around to watch my father fight, betting on it, buying beer and cheering." He was silent again and so was Emma, watching the picture that John had conjured up.

Then he spoke again, more cheerfully. "One thing, though. If Luke's right, then Father fought Jack O'Brien with one hand."

"One hand?"

"When he met Mother he was recovering from the wound he got at Queenston Heights, the wound to his arm. Even when he died the arm was still weak. So when he fought O'Brien it probably wasn't much use at all. Gosh!"

All Emma's hatred of violence surged up. "So the spectators came to see a one-armed man fight," she said bitterly.

"Fight with boots and fists, according to Luke O'Brien. Even if Father won, it would be a dirty business. No wonder he and Mother moved away from York so soon afterward."

"Father must have won!"

She would have liked to know whether this was hero-worship or whether John had reasoned that the winner would have been the one who got Anne Taylor. But before she could say anything, John spoke again.

"I wonder if Mother was . . . was pregnant after Jack O'Brien . . ." He looked up at Emma again and the lantern light showed that he was staring at her speculatively.

For a moment Emma was too shocked by the implication to say anything, but then she remembered something that she did know for a fact. "There was another baby before me – born dead. He was buried beyond the vegetable garden, but Mother and Father told me that they hadn't ever wanted to put up a marker, that they preferred to think of their living children." She choked on the last words, thinking again of the dead parents and of the two babies who had died with them in the fire.

After a while, John asked, "Did Mother and Father ever come back to York for a visit, do you know?"

"Father came once, when *his* father was dying. There were things to be settled. But Mother never wanted to see York again, I think. She sometimes used to joke about having no past life."

"It's easy to see why."

When she was in bed that night, Emma cried bitterly – cried for the poor old man, for the shame and misery of her mother, for her parents' courage in joining their damaged lives and beginning anew at the very edge of the wilderness.

And she cried because the things she had been discovering about her parents seemed to have made strangers of them. No longer could she remember her mother and father as she had known them on the farm; to that she had to add uncouth, violent images that were hard to reconcile with the cheerful, dignified, intelligent people she had known. None of it fitted! In the terrifying and ugly muddle she had lost her parents, lost them *again*.

As her stormy weeping at last exhausted itself, however, and she lay huddled under the covers, her eyes open on total blackness, something emerged from the chaos. The new life that Anne and Martin Anderson had been trying to create for themselves and their children was built on the ruins of their old lives. It was not really a muddle but a rebuilding, just as Emma's present life was a laborious reconstruction on the uninhabitable wreckage of the life that had ended with the farmhouse fire. And, as though something flipped around in her mind, she suddenly saw Martin and Anne as people, not as parents – as people whom she would very much have liked to know.

That started her crying again. But this time it was less bitterly, more in relief at having found her parents again and in seeing a link between her life and theirs. After all, a network of subtle connections existed: connections between her parents and the Heatheringtons starting new lives on the same piece of land – and, most immediately, stronger connections than ever between her and John. It was to those connections that she must hold fast.

EIGHTEEN

An Opportunity

The beginning of the following week brought a spell of almost wintry weather. Day after day there was a cold wind and the sky was constantly overcast. By Thursday the wind carried sleet with it.

All the same, Emma went out in the afternoon. Free time was precious and she always tried to spend it outside the hotel. As usual, she went to King Street to look at the book lying open in the window of Mr. Lesslie's store. As she turned away she bumped into another figure cloaked and hooded against the weather. It was Miss Morgan, who exclaimed, "Goodness, isn't it an awful day!"

"Yes, dreadful." Having no particular destination, Emma thought she might walk along with Miss Morgan for a short distance. "How are the preparations for the school going?"

"Quite well, although there are the usual snags. The land-lord made some objections to my wanting to use the building for a school, but I think I've appeased him. It's surprising what a few extra dollars will do. Look here, I'm on my way there now to take measurements for the curtains. You can come along and hold the other end of the tape – if you have the time?"

"I'd like to. Of course I have to be back at the hotel to help prepare dinner."

"Oh, you will be. Come along."

They crossed Yonge Street and walked west for a couple of blocks, then north. Neither of them spoke; all their energy was needed to cope with their flapping cloaks and to watch their footing in the mud.

At last Miss Morgan led the way up a few steps and unlocked a door. "Heavens, it's good to get indoors out of that wind!" she said, shaking herself and throwing back the hood. "I'd start a fire to warm us up but we won't be here very long."

Emma would have welcomed a fire. Her hands felt stiff and clumsy with the cold. Her feet, wet from the mud that had seeped through her boots, had no feeling at all. She didn't have a muff, as Miss Morgan did, and her cloak was thin and inadequate for this weather.

But she looked about her with interest. The house was empty and very cold, and the wind drummed against it, but it was clean and the inside walls were painted white. Miss Morgan showed her around. On the ground floor there was a good-sized room on each side of the passage and a smaller room and kitchen behind. Above were three quite reasonable bedrooms and two tiny ones. From the back windows could be seen a dreary and unkempt yard littered with junk and dead leaves. The only outbuilding was a privy.

They returned to the front downstairs rooms. "These will be the schoolrooms, of course, one for classes and one for quiet study. I'm having a carpenter make two long tables and four benches." She took a tape measure and pencil and paper out of her muff. "Now you can help me hold the tape."

"When do you plan to open?" Emma asked.

"In January . . . sometime in January," said Miss Morgan, noting down the width of a window. "I've ordered slates and maps and a few books, and I want to have them and the furniture here so that when parents come to talk to me they will see how everything is. As soon as the lease was signed I sent for my belongings – they were still in New Hampshire. And I'm looking about for some furniture for my own rooms. Second-hand furniture is in very short supply here in York." But she spoke cheerfully, as though the lack of furniture were a trifling matter.

"At least the house is clean," Emma remarked a little later.

"Oh, I've had a charwoman and a painter in. You should have seen it when I found it."

When they reached the upstairs rooms, Miss Morgan said, "By December I should be able to set the opening date. Then I'll put notices in the newspapers. I intend to begin living here myself as soon as I have the essential furniture – it will be cheaper than staying at the hotel and will look better to the parents of prospective pupils."

"We'll miss you at the hotel," Emma said, "but at least you'll still be in York." She would have liked to ask whether she might come and visit Miss Morgan at the school sometimes. Just now, though, she was in quest of other information.

"Will you have anyone living here with you – a friend or someone to help with the teaching? You have enough bedrooms."

"I may need those for girls from outlying places who wish to board here, although I'm starting with day pupils only. And I certainly won't need an assistant unless the school grows very much larger than I expect it to. Of course I'll need a servant – a girl-of-all-work at the start and later, when I can afford it, a cook and a maid."

"And someone in the garden?"

"I plan to hire a man to come and clean it up first, and then probably get someone occasionally by the day. There won't be enough work for a full-time boy or man." She jotted down another measurement and then, brooding over the piece of paper, she said almost absentmindedly, "Domestic help is rather scarce here. Nobody wants to be a servant who can set up on his own."

Suddenly she turned and half sat on a window sill, the tape measure and paper gathered in both hands in her lap. She looked straight at Emma who was standing in the middle of the room, her cloak pulled around her against the penetrating cold.

"You wouldn't care to leave the hotel and come to work for me, would you?"

At first Emma barely grasped the significance of the words. She had been gazing out of the window and thinking that if she were Miss Morgan she would make this room, with its view of a fragment of the lake, her own bedroom. Miss Morgan's words hung in the air, then repeated themselves in Emma's mind – *leave the hotel and come to work for me . . . ?*

She looked at Miss Morgan, seeing with startling clarity

the hair mussed by enthusiasm and the weather, the eager face with the question still on it.

"Are you . . . are you offering me a job?" Emma ventured, not really believing it and hearing the shakiness of her own voice.

"It occurred to me to ask. You're interested in the school. It wouldn't be an advancement for you, of course. You'd have to do all the housework except that I'd probably get a charwoman in once a week for the heavy work. You'd do the daily cleaning, the marketing, and the cooking. I suppose you can cook a bit?"

"Only simple things. My mother was teaching me when she died. I'm not at all experienced."

"You'll learn quickly. I've got a cookery book coming with my other belongings. And I'd have time to do some of the cooking myself. I did some at home – we were not at all a grand family. But of course you don't have to decide straight away."

"I'd live here, of course?"

"Yes, you could have one of those small rooms at the back."

"But there's John, my brother. I don't suppose you could use a boy to carry wood and water, clean boots, and so on?"

Miss Morgan thought it over. "Well, as I said before, I hadn't planned to hire a boy or man full time."

That made Emma realize the implications of being the only servant except for the once-weekly charwoman. She, Emma, would have to do not only the work she did now at the hotel but also the carrying in of firewood and water, the taking out of slops, probably the laundry – all the heavier work that the Tubbs did at the hotel. But this gave Emma an idea. "You need not hire John full time. He has a job now in Mr. Blackwood's livery stable but he does some chores in the hotel each morning before he starts work. If he moved here with me he could do the same thing – bring in firewood and water, clear the snow off the steps in winter – in return for his board and room."

"It's a possibility," Miss Morgan said. "How old is your brother?"

"He'll be twelve in a few weeks. He's a good, quick boy, quite grown up and independent for his age."

Miss Morgan lifted herself from the window sill. "Well, there's no hurry for either of us. I wouldn't need you until shortly before the school opened. What is Mrs. McPhail paying you?"

"Two dollars a month – and my board and room, of course – and my working clothes." She spread her cloak to show the black dress underneath. "They're the only ones I have."

"I could pay that. And you might pick up some scraps of education here and there."

Miss Morgan locked the door and they struggled back toward the hotel, hardly speaking. But Emma was exulting inside. She had been offered another job! She could get away from Mrs. McPhail! True, Miss Morgan would not need her until January, but the prospect would be there before her. In that time she could learn more about cooking and marketing, and perhaps spend her free afternoons helping Miss Morgan get settled.

They had almost reached the livery stable when Miss Morgan said, "Your brother works at Blackwood's, didn't you say?"

"Yes, it's just up here."

"I'd like to meet him. Do you think we could have a word with him now?"

This was a good sign. "I'll go and see if he's in. Perhaps, though, you should stay outside the gate. Mr. Blackwood has a window overlooking . . ."

"Quite right. I'll wait here."

Emma saw John at once; he was in the drive shed sweeping out a carriage. He spotted Emma and came at her beckoning.

"Hello, John," said Miss Morgan when Emma had made the introductions. Miss Morgan addressed him in that straightforward, businesslike way that Emma admired. "I've offered Emma a job working for me at the school I'm starting. She would do the housework and cooking – and live in, of course. You could come with her – keep your job here but have your room and board with me in return for doing a few outdoor chores before going to work."

He looked from one to the other in a calm, assessing way. "Like I'm doing now at the hotel?"

"That's right," said Miss Morgan.

"It wouldn't make much difference to me then. I don't mind where I live. So it all depends on Emma. I'd be happy to stay at the hotel with her or move to the school, whatever she decides."

"If you both came to the school," Miss Morgan said, "You'd be company for each other."

This cast a shadow over Emma's spirits, just when she was picturing herself having pleasant evening conversations with Miss Morgan or friendly sessions with her in the kitchen as they did the cooking.

"We don't have to decide right away," she said to John. "Miss Morgan wouldn't need me until January."

"And in any case," said the older lady, "it's too cold out here to talk."

So they took their leave of John and trudged the rest of the way home.

For Emma, that evening's work at the hotel was subtly transformed by the fact that she saw it as something that she might be leaving – that she *would* leave if she decided to accept Miss Morgan's offer. She saw the routine with new eyes, and also watched herself doing what was by now thoroughly familiar. It seemed far longer than a month since she had first waited on table and trembled before the strangeness of the work and the people.

At the same time, another part of her mind was thinking about the school, wondering what it would be like to work for girls, to be the only indoor servant except for the cleaning woman, to sit alone with John in the kitchen in the evenings, to arrange everything to suit herself – and, of course, Miss Morgan.

After finishing her work, she talked to John. They sat on her bed, wrapped in her quilt, with one candle on the shelf opposite them. Through the cracks around the window came enough draft to whip the candle flame and make the light dance wildly; the roof and walls were fragile protection against the weather, which raged only inches from them.

"What do you think of Miss Morgan's offer?" Emma asked.

"Do you expect that she'll make a success of this school?" he countered.

Emma pondered, then told him what she knew about Miss Morgan.

"You like her?" he asked.

"Yes, I do. She's sensible and straightforward. I think her school will succeed. At least it should."

"Are you taking the job?"

She was silent for so long that after a while he said, "You can, you know, without it affecting me. I'll come along and live there – and for the rest I'd be doing just what I do now." After a pause he added, "I like working at Blackwood's."

He looked up at her with a detached, faintly curious expression and, without warning, a wave of desolation swept over Emma. Her difficulties and dissatisfaction were not shared by anybody. No one could see the problem from her angle. What she decided now would probably change her life – just as the decision she had made a month ago, to come to York with Mrs. McPhail rather than stay in Flamborough Township and eventually marry Isaac Bates, had helped to make her what she was now. Grimly, and without conscious thought, she stared at the quarter-pie window, which was black except for the dim reflections from the bedroom – reflections that shook as the wind rattled the glass.

A particularly fierce gust brought her back to her surroundings. She began removing the quilt. "It's time you were in bed."

"I guess so." John yawned enormously, then clambered off the bed. "You too. After all, Father told me to look after you."

"What's that? He said I was to look after *you*. When he sent us out of the house to save us from the fire."

"Oh, well, he told me earlier, when he and I were in the bush one day and saw traces of bear. We joked about bears eating people and then, not joking, he said that, if anything happened to him, I was to look after the family. It . . . it sounded important."

"It is important."

She felt comforted, a little, but no closer to a decision.

All next day Emma fretted over the problem. As she did her work in the hotel, she imagined going through a similar routine in the school: making beds, emptying chamber pots – and also, at the school, cooking meals, washing dishes, shopping for food. She would be able to arrange it to suit herself, though probably the school's needs would leave her little real freedom. Would the fact that she was working in a school actually make any difference? Would she be any less a servant because it was a school rather than a hotel where she worked?

There was a definite appeal in the thought of being free of Mrs. McPhail – except in their roles as guardian and ward – but that meant also being away from Mrs. Jones. As the only servant, she would be alone most of the day. For the first time she saw that independence might well lead to loneliness. True enough, John would be there in the early morning and part of the evening, and the shopping would bring her into contact with people.

So she went through the day, her mind working on two levels. By the evening she was exhausted and confused. She would dearly have loved to talk to someone but dared not reveal that she was considering leaving McPhail's Hotel. Besides, this decision, like the other important ones, had to be made by her alone.

The next morning it was snowing. As always, the first snowfall lifted Emma's spirits, even though at this time of year it was almost certain to melt away again. Over breakfast Major Heatherington discussed the weather with Mrs. McPhail. Emma, listening as she worked, remembered that the Heatheringtons would move to the farm as soon as there was enough snow on the ground for sleigh travel. The thought of their departure depressed her, partly because she would miss them and partly because she was worried about their moving to the farm in winter and alone. Of course the neighbors would help, but still Emma was anxious.

Later that morning, however, she heard a piece of news that partly solved this problem.

"The Berrys have found work," Mrs. Jones announced. "Permanent, I mean." Mr. Berry had been working this week with Joseph, helping to repair the woodshed and the privy, but that was only temporary.

"Really?" Emma asked. "What sort of work?"

"The Heatheringtons're hiring them and taking them to their new farm."

"But . . ." began Emma, intending to protest that there was nowhere on the farm for the Berry family to live. She was glad to have caught herself in time: of course she was not supposed to have any such detailed knowledge.

Mrs. Jones looked up. "But what?"

Emma improvised. "Are the Heatheringtons familiar with . . . with Mrs. Berry's personality?"

To Emma's amazement, Mrs. Jones blushed rather prettily and looked confused. "They asked me about that. Mrs. McPhail told 'em that Mrs. Berry worked for me last week. I warned Mrs. Heatherington that Mrs. Berry's got a will and a tongue but . . . well, you know, I had to say that she was a hard worker. She is, you know, Emma. She don't seem to know what it is to be tired."

"Well, that's good, then," Emma said rather lamely. And of course Mrs. Jones was right. Mrs. Berry's tongue had given no trouble during the preparations for the dinner. "The Heatheringtons are taking the whole Berry family, of course."

"Yes. Mr. Berry'll do the farm work. I think myself that they're pretty lucky to be took on like that."

It was from Mrs. Heatherington that Emma heard more details. "We explained to Mrs. Berry that there was no proper house for them but there is the barn. It's a good barn, better than many laborers' cottages in the old country, and we plan to install a stove for heat. The Major was perfectly fair with them and they agreed to come. I must say I'm relieved to be going out there with servants – I was afraid that otherwise we wouldn't have much heart for it and . . . and perhaps that we wouldn't get off to a good start." She made a restless movement in her chair. "You must have thought us very foolish in the beginning, Emma."

This came so close to the truth that Emma did not know how to answer it. Before she could think of something tactful, Mrs. Heatherington went on.

"You see, my husband and I had an image in our minds – something made up of our own dreams, I suppose, and of the more glowing accounts of travelers. When we heard less favorable reports of conditions here, we dismissed them as prejudiced or inaccurate. After we arrived we were kept busy with the social life of the officers and the well-off local people. Everything conspired to keep us from making contact with real settlers. And then . . . well, we might have been able to buy a farm nearer York, in a less primitive state, if we hadn't had some rather unexpected expenses. . . ."

Emma remembered the big dinner. Launching Caroline in York society, perhaps doing so with extra lavishness to make up for what might be considered their neglect of her in former years, had forced the parents to alter their own plans and expectations.

Mrs. Heatherington seemed to square her shoulders. "From now on we will be more realistic. Actually we are quite looking forward to the challenge. In the summer we are planning to build two houses, one for the Berrys and one for us – joined to each other, the Major thinks, and with a shared kitchen. While the men spend most of the time building, Mrs. Berry and I will do the gardening."

"It sounds like a good arrangement," Emma said, though privately wondering whether the "gardening" would provide enough food for the following winter. All the same, the Berrys would be companions as well as servants and their presence would make the Heatheringtons less vulnerable.

When she went to bed that night, Emma realized that her decision had been made. She had hardly thought about it during the day but she knew now that she would stay in the hotel. It was a more secure position than the one in the school and held at least a chance of improvement if Mrs. Delaney were to leave. There was companionship in the kitchen – and it might even be possible to continue her contact with Miss Morgan and borrow books occasionally. As for education – well, she'd see what came of the Mechanics' Institute that Miss Morgan had mentioned. She acknowledged to herself that when, in the past, she had longed to be able to go to school, she had not been thinking of working in one as a servant.

She took a few more days to consider her decision but did not change it. At length she told Miss Morgan, who took it very calmly. Emma mentioned her worries about being lonely.

"I quite understand," Miss Morgan said. "You're rather young to be by yourself, and of course I would be too busy to be much company for you."

Then Emma wondered whether to tell Mrs. McPhail. There was no real reason for doing so but she dreaded having her aunt hear about the matter in some other way – as, with her sources of information, she probably would. So one afternoon she tapped on her aunt's door. As she did, she realized that this was almost the first time that *she* had gone to talk with Mrs. McPhail.

"Come in."

She went in.

Mrs. McPhail was sitting at her desk going over Mrs. Jones' kitchen accounts. She laid down her pencil and gestured Emma to the chair.

"I wanted to . . . to tell you about something that has recently occurred," Emma began, nervous as usual in Mrs. McPhail's presence even though she had rehearsed what she was going to say.

"Yes?"

"Miss Morgan offered me a position in her school as cook and general servant."

"And you wished to discuss it with me? Very wise, since I am your guardian." There was a faintly sardonic note in Mrs. McPhail's voice, but for once Emma was not hurt or frightened by it. It was, in fact, almost playful.

"No. To tell you that I decided not to accept."

Mrs. McPhail was silent and her face thoughtful as she looked at Emma. "Well, well. You're taking matters into your own hands."

"They *are* in my own hands, Mrs. McPhail, whether I like it or not. Since my parents died . . ."

"But as your guardian I stand in their place." It was put forward less as a decree than as a point for debate. Emma registered the difference in manner but had to concentrate on the discussion.

"I'm sorry, but it doesn't *feel* like that. Legally I guess we have to have a guardian, but . . ." How could she explain that she would never be able to take all the large and small questions and interests of life to her aunt as she had taken them to her parents? She could not think of a way to say it without hurting Mrs. McPhail's feelings.

That thought startled Emma. Never before had she worried about Mrs. McPhail's feelings. But this interview had developed in an unexpected way. Emma had never seen her aunt so open, so unofficial. Even now there was nothing especially kindly or soft or maternal about her, but Emma caught a glimpse of another woman – the one behind the controlled face – who would be a good friend or an interesting companion to the people she liked. Curious that this glimpse should come just as Emma was declaring that she did not feel as close to Mrs. McPhail as she had to her parents. Even now Mrs. McPhail was not a comfortable person, but she was an interesting human being.

"Yes, I think I understand that," Mrs. McPhail said, and Emma had to scramble around to recall the remark to which this was the answer. "We have, after all, not known each other very long." She paused for a moment and then gave a restrained but not unfriendly smile. "You are a very independent young lady. So was I, at your age. In that way at least we are kin."

Emma was so astounded by this that she could only manage a smile in return, and then it was a smile tremulous with surprise and pleasure at being called a young lady and at being treated to such a confidence.

Mrs. McPhail picked up her pencil. "I hope you will not regret staying in your present position," she said. Her usual manner had returned, but Emma would not forget the contact that had been made today, the insight she had gained. "And I may as well tell you now that this evening Mrs. Delaney and I both have to go out and I'd like you to be on duty in the lobby, as you were once before."

"Yes, ma'am."

"For this occasion it will not be necessary to wear an apron."

Emma's eyes widened. "No apron of any kind?"

"You will have more authority without one. It is merely a matter of business and of the hotel's image in the eyes of the customers."

"Yes, Mrs. McPhail."

After dinner Emma went upstairs to tidy her hair before spending the evening in the lobby. As she took off her apron and smoothed her dress, she felt as though she had, in that one day, grown up by another jump. Being called a young lady by Mrs. McPhail was an enormous improvement – and so was the glimpse of her aunt's inner personality. Standing in front of the quarter-pie window – using it as a mirror because it was larger than the looking glass over the washstand – she realized that something else very important had happened. She was now in the hotel by choice rather than from compulsion. She had had the offer of a position elsewhere but had chosen to stay.

When she was about to leave the room she paused to touch the tinderbox, her legacy and talisman from the past, and send a little thought to her parents. She touched Mrs. Heatherington's ink bottle, which pointed toward the future. Then she went downstairs with brisk steps to her post in the lobby.